HORSES OF

HALF MOON
RANCH

WILD HORSES

WILD HORSES

JENNY OLDFIELD

Illustrated by
Paul Hunt

Hodder
Children's
Books

a division of Hodder Headline plc

With thanks to Bob, Karen and Katie Foster, and to the staff and
guests at Lost Valley Ranch, Deckers, Colorado

First published in Great Britain in 1999
by Hodder Children's Books

The right of Jenny Oldfield to be identified as the author of
this work has been asserted by her in accordance with the
Copyright, Designs and Patents Act 1988.

10 9 8 7 6 5 4 3 2 1

A Catalogue record for this book is available from the British Library

ISBN 0 340 71616 9

Typeset by Avon Dataset Ltd, Bidford-on-Avon, Warks

Printed and bound in Great Britain by
The Guernsey Press Co. Ltd, Channel Isles

Hodder Children's Books
a division of Hodder Headline plc
338 Euston Road
London NW1 3BH

1

Kirstie Scott felt the bounce in Lucky's stride. His head was up, ears flicking to left and right as she relaxed in the saddle and gave him plenty of rein.

'Let's head for Miners' Ridge,' Charlie Miller called from the front. He reined his horse to the right and led the group of seven riders along a narrow trail between silver aspen trees.

Great! Kirstie smiled to herself and nudged Lucky on with her legs. Miners' Ridge, at the end of Meltwater Trail, was one of her favourite treks out from Half-Moon Ranch. It would take them by the banks of rushing creeks and waterfalls, through spooky Dead Man's Canyon.

Good! Lucky echoed her mood by picking up his pace. He broke into an easy trot, splashing through a shallow stream to catch up with Charlie and tuck himself in behind Moose, the young wrangler's sturdy grey quarter horse.

Behind them, the other six riders took things more slowly. It was the last Saturday in May; their first day as paying guests at the Scotts' ranch. To them, the steep slopes leading through dark pine forests and beyond that to snow-peaked mountains, were new and risky.

'You gotta trust your horses,' Charlie assured them. 'They know the trail. All you gotta do is stay in line.'

Kirstie grinned over her shoulder at the nervous followers. They were visitors from cities and towns, mostly without much riding experience. Trust your horse; that was the key. With a creak of saddle leather, she turned back and gazed straight ahead.

Sure, it looked difficult. The trail rose sharply, zig-zagging between boulders, overhung by branches. But it looked pretty too. The bright green aspen leaves shook and fluttered in the breeze, a carpet of blue columbines grew around the roots. Summer! Kirstie sighed. After the long, cold Colorado winter of snow and ice, the leaves and the flowers were just great.

Summer was here and school was out. 'Good boy, Lucky!' she murmured as her beautiful palomino picked his way between boulders. His rich golden coat looked dappled in the fluttering shadows, his long, creamy mane hung smoothly down his neck.

No more school through June and July. And her mother had driven to Denver this very morning to pick up Kirstie's big brother, Matt, from college. The family would be together again. Long days to ride the trails. Blue skies and mountains rolling on forever...

'Kirstie?' Charlie broke into her dream.

'Hmm?' She sighed, pushed a wisp of fair hair back from her face, then urged Lucky alongside Moose.

'Can you lead? I need to check on that guy at the back of the line.'

'The one who's riding Silver Flash?' She glanced back at the last rider. The middle-aged man had decided to leave the trail and take a short cut to the front. He'd forced his sorrel-coloured mare off the track and shoved her up against a rocky slope which was impossible for Silver Flash to climb. Now he was digging his heels in hard, grunting and leaning forward in the saddle to make the horse go. 'Sure,' Kirstie told Charlie, as the wrangler went off to sort the man out.

She and Lucky went on with the rest of the group, a woman with two teenage sons, and a young married couple. Up ahead, the trail hit a short, level, sunny patch before it climbed again, this time between the tall, scaly trunks of ponderosa pine.

'This sure is tough going,' the woman behind her remarked as the gloomier trees closed in.

She was riding Johnny Mohawk, a dainty, sure-footed black horse that Kirstie had helped her mother to buy last fall. Kirstie nodded but said nothing.

'I sure do hope the weather holds,' the woman went on, an edge of nervousness in her voice.

Kirstie glanced up. There were glimpses in the distance of clouds gathering over Eagle's Peak; at 13,000 feet the highest mountain around. 'Yep,' she agreed.

'What happens if it rains? Do we turn back and head for the ranch house?'

'Nope.' Kirstie didn't like to talk much while she rode. She preferred silence; to hear the stiff, dry rustle of the pine needles as the wind drove through the trees, to breathe in the sharp woody smells and look out for chipmunks or ground squirrels scurrying on ahead of the horses' plodding feet.

So she was glad when Charlie came back up front. 'I tell you one thing for sure,' he muttered in Kirstie's ear as he rode by on Moose. 'Some horses are much smarter than your average dude.'

She grinned back at him. 'Silver Flash is a pretty smart horse,' she agreed, pleased to see that horse and dude rider were back in line. She and Charlie often shared a joke. He was 19 years old, a year younger than her brother, Matt, and had come to work at Half-Moon just after Christmas. Tall and dark, with cropped, black hair, he wore a thick, big-checked blue and white shirt, worn-out jeans and battered cowboy boots.

'How long before we reach Miners' Ridge?' the nervous woman on Johnny Mohawk asked now, one eye still on the distant rain clouds.

Charlie rode Moose steadily on, waiting to answer until after he'd helped his horse pick his way across a splashing stream. Then he turned in his saddle and yelled over the sound of the water. 'The whole ride should take us three hours or thereabouts.' Pointing to the track of the stream, he showed them where he planned to lead them. 'See there, up by the fall? The trail heads off to the left, up to Hummingbird Rock. And past that, you see where the two cliffs meet in a narrow pass?'

The group of visitors scrunched up their faces, peered up the hill at the rocky horizon, then nodded.

'That's Dead Man's Canyon. We get through there, up on to the ridge until we come across the opening to an old goldmine. And that's when we start heading for home.' Charlie grinned, then reined Moose to the left, on up the slope.

It was Kirstie's turn to take Lucky through the

racing stream. She leaned back in the saddle as he strode down the bank, heard the clunk of his hooves as they hit the rocky bed. The white, foaming water splashed up around her boots and jeans. 'Trust your horse.' She heard Charlie's advice inside her head and let Lucky find his own way across. The palomino's hooves slid and clunked, found solid ground, trod safely on. Ten seconds later, they were through the stream and climbing up the far bank.

Ten *minutes* later, after much urging and encouraging from Charlie, the six visitors had also made it.

'A little wet around the ankles,' Johnny Mohawk's rider, Loretta, complained. 'But worth it!'

She smiled at Kirstie and Kirstie smiled back.

'You know something?' Loretta confided as the group rode on through the ponderosas towards Dead Man's Canyon.

'Nope,' Kirstie replied, swinging her hair behind her shoulders with a quick toss of her head.

'I never thought I'd say this when we first came on the trail. I mean, I was pretty darned scared back there . . .' She settled into her saddle, tucked in behind Lucky, heading for the tall, grey cliff faces that formed the narrow canyon.

'Say what?' Kirstie glanced back at the slight, pale-faced woman with short, dark hair. Her face was excited and kind of lit up at having crossed the tricky stream. There was a light in Kirstie's own large, grey eyes. She'd just guessed what Loretta was about to confess.

'This week here at Half-Moon Ranch; I think it's gonna be a whole lot of fun!'

Fun and tons of hard work for the family who ran it, Kirstie thought. She settled back into listening to the wind in the trees as she ended her talk with Loretta and rode on.

Kirstie had left the city and moved here with her mother and brother just four years ago, when she was nine years old. 'Here' was at the end of a five mile dirt road off Route 3 out of San Luis, a small town of one main street, a grocery store and a gas station, which was another ten miles down the paved road. 'Here' was 8,000 feet up in the Rocky Mountains, in the Meltwater Range, and it was uphill all the way to Wyoming. Fifteen miles to school each day; three and a half hours by car to Denver, where she'd once lived.

That had been when her dad had still been part of their family, and her grandma and grandpa had run Half-Moon Ranch, grazing a few hundred longhorn cattle in the green valley by Five Mile Creek.

Then, in one terrible year, when she was eight, it had all fallen apart. Her dad had left home suddenly; almost, it seemed to Kirstie, without a word of warning. One day he was there, driving into his office in the city. The next day, the Good Friday before Easter, he'd packed his bags and gone, leaving a hole where he'd once been, an empty place at the table, a space in the garage, no one in the big double bed beside her mom.

Matt, Kirstie and Sandy Scott. No Glen Scott. Their dad had a new girlfriend, a new life. His picture was in the silver frame on the bookshelf. That was all.

That weekend they had driven out to Half-Moon Ranch to be with Grandma and Grandpa. Kirstie's mom had gone around the log-built ranch house in dazed silence, while Kirstie and Matt rode out with Grandpa to bring in some early calves. It set the pattern for that first, lonely summer; driving out of town at weekends, away from the emptiness of their Denver home, to a place where nothing ever changed.

Only it did. Kirstie had just turned nine when, sudden as her dad's leaving, Grandpa fell ill and died of a heart attack. And this time she didn't even have a chance to say goodbye. The old man had been out working the cattle. It was their farmhand, Hadley Crane, who came riding back to Grandma with the news.

They called out the doctor from San Luis, but by the time he got there it was way too late.

People at the funeral said it was how old Chuck Glassner would have wanted to die: suddenly, out working the cattle by the side of Five Mile Creek. That puzzled Kirstie: she knew her grandpa would never have wanted to leave his ranch, his wife, his daughter and grandchildren – he loved them all too much.

But now, four years later, she was beginning to understand. She ran through those years as the shadows of Dead Man's Canyon began to close down on the small group of horses and riders. She remembered the day when they'd shut up the neat, modern house in Denver and moved out to Half-Moon Ranch for good.

Sandy Scott had decided to take the gamble of leaving the city with her two kids and setting up home and business on the eastern slopes of the Colorado Rockies. With Grandma's blessing, they were going to turn the cattle ranch into a small vacation centre for paying guests. There were five cabins to build in the aspen trees that sheltered the original ranch house; small log houses with open fires, sitting-rooms and bedrooms where visitors would be comfortable.

That took a year of hard work from Hadley and another cowhand, who had stayed on after Grandpa's death. Then there were horses to buy at the horse sale barn in San Luis – Hadley again, though by this time Sandy herself had developed a good eye for the points of a horse. She planned ahead, bought wisely, waited for Hadley and a couple of local men to build a sound corral, strong tack-room and feeding-stalls.

Then, two summers ago, Half-Moon had finally opened its doors to paying guests.

Kirstie took a deep breath at the memory of her mom's face as she'd welcomed their first visitors. It had been nervous, with small frown marks between her fair eyebrows, and she'd been too brisk in showing them to their cabins . . .

Just then Lucky tensed beneath the saddle, picking up his rider's momentary edginess. His ears flicked round, quizzing Kirstie. What's the problem? Was it something I did?

'Not you,' she murmured. She clicked her tongue gently against the roof of her mouth to urge him on. 'It was me. I was just . . . thinking.' She sighed again.

The winter before last had been her grandma's time to fall ill. In Kirstie's mind, the old lady seemed to fade with the light. As days grew shorter, nights longer and colder, and the aspen leaves had turned from bright gold to brown, her gran had grown more frail. This time there was no surprise; Kirstie knew she would die.

'I've seen you build this place from nothing,' Grandma had told Sandy in her last days. 'I've seen you work and build a whole new life out here. I'm so proud.'

She had slid away from them, died peacefully, and Kirstie's sadness, though strong, was less sharply painful than at the other two terrible times.

These things had made her quieter than she was before, less likely to rely on people being there for her when she needed them. And now, when she looked at her mom and the growing success of the ranch, she could believe that a person could make anything happen, if only they wanted it enough. It made her feel good . . . That, and the horses of Half-Moon Ranch.

Lucky, Moose, Johnny Mohawk and Silver Flash. Crazy Horse and Cadillac, her brother Matt's favourite. More than a dozen horses of all colours: sorrel, fleabitten grey, palomino and Appaloosas; all good American quarter horses, but each with their own personality and special spirit.

Like Silver Flash now; the sorrel horse with the bright white flash down the length of his bony, intelligent face. He knew all too well that he had a complete beginner on his back. The man was heavy, with a dark moustache. His name was

Ronnie Vernon and he worked at a bank in Dallas, Texas. Whenever he tried to dig his heels into Silver Flash's sides to make him break from the line and trot forwards, the smart horse refused to obey.

From up front, Charlie caught sight of Ronnie Vernon's tactics. He sighed and asked Kirstie to head the line once more. 'Don't try to overtake as we get near the canyon!' he yelled at the man, turning Moose and heading down the slope to make sure that his instructions got through.

Meanwhile, Kirstie knew there was another stream to cross before the horses could enter the narrow channel between the rocks into Dead Man's Canyon. Horseshoe Creek was coming up; she could hear the water gushing and tumbling down the rocks around the next bend in the trail.

'Sounds kind of full,' Loretta said, still following close on Lucky's heels.

'That would be the snow melting from the mountain tops,' Kirstie explained. 'It all runs down into Five Mile Creek and on into Big Bear River. This time of year there's always a lot of water.'

She and Lucky rounded the bend first, to find

the creek leaping and swirling its way between wet black rocks. It tumbled over tree trunks that had fallen across its path, and sent white spray drifting towards them.

'Wow!' One of Loretta's sons pulled Cadillac to a sudden halt. The big, creamy-white horse tossed his head and skittered sideways. Back down the line, everyone stopped.

'It's OK. Follow me.' Kirstie had made this crossing dozens of times before, and she knew the safest place. It was only the wild sound of the water surging between the rocks that made it seem more difficult than it really was.

Lucky knew this too. He went boldly forward to the water's edge, dropped his head, and with his ears pricked forward, stepped into the fast-running stream.

Kirstie's horse was strong and certain. She knew he would pick his way through. And she loved the feel of the ice-cold spray on her hands and face as Lucky steadied himself, then went on, picking up his feet to step over a fallen log, letting the torrent push against his sturdy legs without giving way.

'Good boy!' Kirstie leaned forward to pat his

neck as Lucky stepped up the far bank. Now they must wait for Loretta to pluck up the courage to try. 'Come on, it's fine!' she called back. 'Give Johnny Mohawk his head and let him do it for you!'

She watched the dainty black horse put a first foot in the water, and noticed that, right at the back of the line, Charlie had finally got Ronnie Vernon in order.

The wrangler gave her a wave and yelled at her to go ahead into the canyon. 'We'll meet up with you there!'

So Kirstie watched Loretta through, then urged Lucky on, glad to let Charlie take charge once more. And she picked up an eagerness in her horse too. He seemed to be in a hurry, putting more pace into his walk. She clicked and he broke into a trot. 'What is it?' she murmured. 'What have you heard?'

Lucky's ears were forward, his head up, as they entered Dead Man's Canyon. A wind whipped through his pale mane and his golden shoulders grew dark with sweat as they left the group behind.

'You heard something,' Kirstie acknowledged, tensing a little. Or was it just the wind and the darkening sky that had made Lucky quicken his pace? Those distant clouds over Eagle's Peak were speeding towards them, drawing down on to Miners' Ridge, bringing rain. 'Easy, boy!' she whispered, holding him back from a lope.

The rocks to either side rose sheer and blocked what was left of the sun. The shadows closed in.

And then she saw.

Lucky stopped dead. And Kirstie discovered what it was that had made him so eager to push ahead.

A herd of horses had gathered at the far end of the canyon. Horses without headcollars, their manes tangled, heads up, tails swishing a warning to the intruders. Beautiful sorrels, dazzling greys, paints and Appaloosas. Horses that had never been broken to wear bridle or bit.

Wild horses. And at their head, watching every move that Kirstie and Lucky made, was their leader. Taller than the rest, with a proud, arched neck and flaring nostril, the black stallion kept guard.

'Easy!' Kirstie whispered to Lucky. The wild horses had penned themselves into a dead end where the walls of the canyon finally met. The only way out was by a steep trail to her right, up on to Miners' Ridge.

The horse was perfect and proud, strong and fierce as he pawed at the ground to warn them away from his herd. His black coat shone, his mane fell forward over his long, wild face.

Holding her breath and not daring to move, Kirstie stared in silence at the beautiful black stallion.

Unflinching under her gaze, the proud horse stared back as the dark clouds rolled towards them, and in the distance, over Eagle's Peak, forked lightning flashed.

2

The stallion stared back at Kirstie and Lucky. His herd milled restlessly in the stony gulley where Dead Man's Canyon came to an abrupt end. Sheer red-brown cliffs towered above them, trapping them. He studied the two possible escape routes; the trail which Kirstie had travelled, or the steep track up the cliffs to Miners' Ridge.

Striking the rocky earth with his front hoof, the stallion tossed his head. He swung angrily towards Lucky, then turned his head and trotted back, corralling his herd deeper into the impassable gulley.

'Easy!' Kirstie breathed. Behind her, Charlie calmed the other trail horses and their uneasy riders. She could feel Lucky's flanks quiver, saw his ears flatten against his neck. A rumble of thunder rolled overhead, setting the palomino's ears still further back. He stepped sideways, tugging at the reins in fright.

Then there was more lightning, this time just above them. A great, forked flash of it tearing through the dark clouds. And drops of cold rain, large and slow at first, spattering on to the rocks and the trapped horses.

Lucky flinched at the electric flash. Thirty metres from where he and Kirstie stood, the black stallion reared. He went up on to his hind legs, his front feet flailing, head back, teeth bared. Another blinding flash, and this time the thunder rolled across the ridge with a clatter and a crack. A wind drove the clouds down the snow-topped mountain in a torrrent of icy, hard rain.

'Come on, let's get out of here!' Kirstie decided to veer away from the hostile stallion and his frightened herd. In the flashing lightning and crashing thunder, it must seem to them that she and Lucky were blocking their escape. So she reined Lucky to the left, hoping to leave the way clear for the wild horses to reach the track on to the ridge.

But then, before the stallion could pick up her good intention, there was the sound of more hooves drumming behind them. A blurred shape appeared in the rain at the mouth of the canyon; a man on horseback galloping at full speed.

Surprised, holding Lucky on a tight rein, Kirstie peered through the sheet of rain. She made out the heavy figure of Ronnie Vernon on Silver Flash. The horse was out of control, no doubt spooked by his clumsy rider and by the storm into stampeding ahead of the rest of the group. Clinging to the saddle horn, his jacket flying open, hatless and soaked, Vernon careered towards her.

For a few stunned seconds, Kirstie thought they were headed for a collision. Rapidly she sidestepped Lucky out of the runaway horse's path, heard the wild stallion whinny from the depths of the gulley. Lucky whirled on the spot, testing her balance to the limit.

Then Silver Flash made a decision of his own. He'd spotted the track on to Miner's Ridge. It was a trail he knew well, so he headed for it, regardless of his rider. It was his only way out of this echoing, dark, storm-torn place and he took it.

Steadying Lucky, Kirstie stared after them. Silver Flash's hooves drummed up the narrow track, setting small stones rolling. It was the route she'd wanted the stallion to use, but now the wild herd cowered at the far end of the canyon once more, away from the falling stones. Meanwhile, the rain bounced off the rocks and formed muddy brown streams in the dirt channels, loosening more stones.

'Kirstie!' Charlie's voice yelled from the mouth of the canyon. 'Don't let that rider go any further. It's not safe!'

'Too late!' she yelled back.

Vernon and Silver Flash were fifty metres up the slope, now dislodging bigger stones that crashed over the edge of the track and landed on the canyon floor. One missed the black stallion by less than a metre. He reared up and sideways as it crashed down, his wet mane straggled across a neck that was flecked with white spots of sweat.

'Then look out for yourself and get out of there!' Charlie called. He'd ridden after Vernon as far as the mouth of Dead Man's Canyon and taken in the scene through the sheet of rain; Kirsty and Lucky to one side, the wild herd at the far end, and the cliff track crumbling under Silver Flash's hooves as Vernon rode him high on to the ridge.

'What about the wild horses?' she cried.

'Never mind them. Just get out as fast as you can!'

Behind Charlie, Kirstie made out a huddle of riders. He was right; she had to get out quick. The sooner she and Lucky left the canyon, the easier it would be for the black stallion to lead the herd out too. So she kicked Lucky into action. For some reason he wouldn't go. She kicked again.

'Get a move on!' Charlie shouted, his voice hoarse.

'I can't! Lucky won't shift!'

More rocks fell; bigger and louder, crowding the wild herd against the wall of the canyon. Overhead, Silver Flash was scrambling up the last stretch of track on to the ridge.

Kirstie was soaked to the skin, rainwater running

from her scalp, down her face, dripping through her shirt on to her shoulders and back, drenching her jeans. 'Come on, Lucky, please!'

Nothing. He stood like the statue of a horse in the eye of the storm.

And then, as if in slow motion, the lines and contours around her changed shape. The actual land shifted. Only Lucky stayed still as every inch of rock tilted and slipped.

'Landslide!' Charlie yelled, as if from a great distance. Then his voice was swallowed by the roar of falling rock.

Landslide! The cliff face where Vernon had raced his horse on to the ridge was crumbling. Whole chunks of brown rock were breaking away and tumbling, caving in like sugar under a deluge of muddy water. Uprooted trees swayed and toppled in a din of snapping branches, a blur of green and brown.

Gasping, almost crying, Kirstie pulled Lucky tight into the opposite cliff. No wonder the poor horse had refused to move. He'd sensed the landslide before she had and kept to the only safe place in the canyon.

The rock fall gathered momentum. The cliff face cracked and disintegrated as a flash of lightning lit up the whole terrifying scene; horses cowering as rocks crumbled and crashed, the black stallion driving them back as they tried to make a crazy dash towards the disappearing cliff.

Still Lucky was frozen with fear. If they stayed in this spot now, a tumbling rock would soon get them. Kirstie decided she must jump off and lead him out of danger.

Throwing her leg over the back of the saddle, she slipped from Lucky's back, grabbed the reins and tried to move him out of danger. There was still time to do as Charlie had said and head for the mouth of the canyon. But they had to be quick. She tugged at the reins and sobbed. 'Come on, Lucky, please!'

Muscles locked, legs planted wide, he refused.

And the rocks kept on coming. They were sliding in muddy heaps, piling up across the exit, blocking their way.

Lucky strained back from the reins, eyes rolling. It was no good; Kirstie couldn't shift him.

Alone she could make it. If she dropped the

reins and scrambled through the debris, she could get out of this death-trap. But it would mean leaving Lucky. She would rather die than do that. Really, she would rather die.

Instead of abandoning her beloved horse to his fate, she dropped the reins and circled her arms around his neck. 'OK,' she sighed. 'You win. We wait here until it's all over.'

'You OK in there?' It was Charlie's voice, muffled by the rockfall that blocked the entrance to Dead Man's Canyon. Other anxious voices backed him up, demanding to know how Kirstie was.

The silence after the shattering crash of rock against rock was eerie. All she could hear was the rain pattering down. Kirstie opened her eyes. 'We're fine!' she called back. All in one piece. No bones broken.

That was a miracle in itself. After she'd thrown her arms around Lucky's neck and waited, the rocks had kept on coming. She'd heard them bounce and splinter, split off in every direction then land with sickening thuds. But not one had touched them or even left a scratch.

'How about Silver Flash?' Charlie asked.

She stared up at the new shape of the cliff. It had jagged chasms, streams and waterfalls where there had once been trees and a thin covering of earth. The fleeing horse and his novice rider were nowhere to be seen. 'I don't know!' she replied in a faint, scared voice.

'Listen, Kirstie; we can't get over this fall of rock to reach you! It's too high, and pretty dangerous by the look of things.' Charlie sounded worried despite her assurance that she and Lucky were OK. 'How is it on your side?'

She took a deep breath and dragged her gaze away from the ragged, uneven ridge. Her eyes swept quickly down the altered rock-face, along the canyon to the narrow gulley. It was difficult to make out shapes in the dust and drizzling rain, but there, at the far end, the herd of wild horses stood in petrified silence. 'Not too bad,' she called to Charlie. 'Except the track up on to the ridge has gone, so it looks like there's no way out.'

'OK.' Charlie obviously needed time to think it through.

There was more silence. Then Kirstie noticed

what she should have spotted straight away. She looked again, through the gloom at the group of ghostly horses. 'There was a wild horse in here; a lead male!' she cried to the listeners beyond the landslide. 'Charlie, the black stallion's gone!'

The shock tore into her. One moment he'd stood there, his black coat streaming with rain, wide-shouldered, deep-chested. His long tail had swung, his feet had stamped. He was protecting his herd. Next moment, the land fell away. Now he was gone.

Had she imagined him? Was he a shadow against the red cliff, a figment of her imagination? Perhaps no real horse could ever have been so perfect.

Kirstie laid a hand on Lucky's neck. He dipped his head and nudged her forward. Then he too took a step across the rock-strewn canyon.

The horses in the wild herd saw them move. They edged nervously away, around the rim of the gulley, all looking grey and unreal through the rain. Ignoring them, Lucky put his head down and headed ten, fifteen metres towards a heap of newly-fallen rocks. Two uprooted pine trees had landed in the shape of a cross beside the unstable pile,

their branches brushing the ground and making a green screen in front of the crumbled cliff face.

Trust your horse. It was the golden rule at Half-Moon Ranch. Lucky knew what he was doing. So Kirstie stepped after him, right up to the screen of broken branches and sharp pine needles, where the palomino had stopped. Pushing past him, she climbed up the heap and pushed the nearest branch to one side.

Her heart lurched again. There, half buried beneath the rockfall, was the stallion.

Kirstie let out a gasp. Straight away, before she could even think, she squatted down and began tearing at the fallen rocks with her hands, heaving them to one side, wrenching with all her might. The horse was motionless, eyes closed, head sunk awkwardly against a ledge, his front legs invisible, but his back legs and hindquarters clear of the landslide.

If she could just move the rocks from his chest and shoulders . . . She tore away, grazing her hands so badly they bled. The scarlet trickles merged with the rain and mud, but she didn't feel the cuts. All that mattered was freeing the stallion.

He was unconscious, but still breathing. She could see his chest heave as she dragged a large rock free. But what about his legs? She went more carefully now, lifting the last rocks from around his girth until she uncovered the long, black front legs. Then she stopped and sat back on her haunches, staring down at a blood-soaked mess. The horse's left knee had been crushed by a heavy rock.

'Kirstie?' Charlie's voice drifted over the barrier of boulders and mud.

She swallowed hard, struggled to control her voice. 'I've found him!'

'The stallion? Is he hurt?'

'Yes.'

'Bad?'

'Pretty bad. Charlie, we need help!' Softly she put out a bleeding hand to touch the stallion. She stroked the soaked black coat, wiped away the dirt from around his mouth and nostrils.

The horse opened his eyes. They flickered shut, then opened again. He lifted his head.

'Easy!' she whispered.

Lucky stepped back to give the wild creature space.

The stallion pulled away from Kirstie's hand. His eyes rolled in fear at the human touch.

'It's OK,' she whispered. 'I won't hurt you.'

But he didn't trust her. He lay on his side, kicking with his back legs, feebly at first, then more strongly as he regained consciousness. He wanted to be up, away from the pile of ugly rocks that had crashed down on to him, away from the girl with bleeding hands, her soaking hair plastered to her skull, her face smeared with mud.

Kirstie held her breath. She wanted to help him on to his feet and he wouldn't let her. Instead, he struggled alone. He got his back legs under him, ready to take his weight and shove. His head was raised. Now his knees should bend and he should roll from his side on to them, then push up until he was standing. But his injured knee buckled under him. Once, twice, he tried but sank back.

'Charlie, fetch help!' Kirstie stood up, took hold of Lucky's reins and together they ran towards the debris that blocked the entrance. 'I don't care how you get in here, just fetch help . . . please!'

'OK. I'll radio to base and take the whole group back to the ranch with me. You hang on, do what you can for him!' The wrangler took the only way out of the mess.

'Don't be long!' she pleaded.

'About an hour and a half,' he promised. 'Just hang on, OK?'

Dragging breath into her lungs to stem the panic that almost choked her, she convinced him that she would be OK. 'Go, Charlie!' she cried.

An hour and a half before anyone came . . . Would her mom and Matt be back from Denver? Could they get the vet over from San Luis? If they did, would the wild stallion let him near? And were his injuries too bad to treat?

Questions crowded into her head and jostled for answers. None came. Meanwhile, as the herd waited uneasily by the far cliff and Lucky stood patiently at a distance, Kirstie knew that it was up to her to calm the injured horse and stop the bleeding from his injured leg.

She turned to face him, his life in her hands.

3

The stallion knew that he was helpless, his magnificent power stripped away by the crashing rocks. As Kirstie went cautiously towards him again, anxious not to distress him, his whole body quivered. His eyes rolled, his nostrils flared.

Behind her, Lucky followed then came to a halt midway between the injured horse and the rest of the herd. His metal shoe struck bare rock and echoed through the canyon making the wild horses shy away in a tight huddle. Without their leader, trapped by the landslide, they turned and swung nervously this way and that.

'Easy, boy!' Kirstie whispered as she approached the bleeding horse.

He was struggling to raise himself, pawing at the ground with his front feet, reaching out his head and straining to take his weight on the injured knee.

'Wait!' Kirstie drew near. She knew horses and some basic first aid, so she planned what to do. The first thing was that the wound needed to be strapped tight to stop the bleeding. If the stallion would let her get close enough. Breathing steady, reassuring words, she advanced step by step.

The horse tossed his head, whipping his wet black mane back from his face. He watched her every move.

If she looked him in the eye, he would see this as a threat, Kirstie knew. So she kept her gaze fixed on the wounded knee. She inched towards him, her eyes averted, murmuring encouragement.

The stallion struggled again, every nerve straining against her approach.

When eventually she was within a few inches of

him, feeling his hot breath on her hand as she knelt and stretched out to touch him, slowly, slowly winning his trust, she decided on her next move.

She was wearing a T-shirt under her denim shirt so, quickly and smoothly, she withdrew her hand and unbuttoned her top shirt. It was soaking wet from the rain, but once she had it off, she was able to pull hard at a seam and tear down the length of one side. Within a minute, the pale blue shirt was in strips, ready to use as a bandage around the stallion's knee.

The horse's head was up, his eyes watchful, his body still quivering with tension and pain. The clink of a bridle and the sound of metal shoes shuffling over rocky ground in the background told Kirstie that Lucky was still wisely keeping a safe distance.

'Here we go!' she breathed, taking one end of the makeshift bandage and edging forward on her knees. Luckily the stallion's left leg was uppermost, the damaged knee clearly on view. Kirstie flinched as she saw the skin scraped back from the bony joint, the jagged, dirty wound and the steady flow of blood on the wet rock where he lay. But she pressed on, determined to lay the bandage across the wound and slip the fabric under the leg so that she could begin winding it and strapping it tight.

'Good boy!' she soothed. Amazingly, a sixth sense must have told the wild creature that she was offering him his only chance of survival. He kept his head up, watching her as she strapped the wound, but he didn't resist.

Kirstie worked quickly. When one length of torn shirt was used up, she began another. At first, blood seeped quickly through each layer, but then the tight padding began to take effect. Soon, the bleeding eased and she was able to secure the bandage in a tight knot.

Taking a deep breath, she sat back on her haunches. Now it was important to get the stallion on his feet. If he stayed down until help arrived, he would lose heart. He had to get up under his own steam. Yet how was she going to help him stand? She looked round, searching for the right idea.

The herd was still milling around in the gulley. Lucky was waiting nearby. If she borrowed his headcollar and halter rope, which the Half-Moon horses sometimes wore under their bits and bridles, she might have the solution.

So she slipped quickly to where Lucky stood and, with hasty fingers, fumbled with the wet straps and buckles. At last she slid the headcollar off and unhitched the halter rope from the side of the saddle horn. Then she ran back to the black stallion.

'Now trust me,' she urged, offering him the headcollar. Of course, he'd never seen anything like this before. Would he take it quietly or resist?

The horse's head drew back from the contraption. Through his pain and confusion, a deep instinct told him that the headcollar was not to be trusted. This was a trap.

'Not for long!' Kirstie whispered. 'I promise!'

With one hand on his neck, she used the other to ease the headcollar towards his soft, grey nose. Again he jerked away. Kirstie insisted. She took her hand from his neck and offered the collar with both hands. This was going to be the only way.

The more the stallion leaned away, the firmer

she became. She urged the collar on to him, talking quietly, easing the straps over his nose and under his throat. Since he couldn't move from the spot where he'd fallen, in the end he had to accept.

The collar was on, buckled tight. The rope trailed across the rocks. The horse shook his head, ears back, hating the feel of the straps.

Getting to her feet, Kirstie judged the best move. It was the left leg that was injured. It now stuck straight out, stiffened by the tight strapping around the knee. But the right knee looked sound. What she had to do was to use the collar and rope to persuade the horse to rise to his feet, taking his weight on the right leg only. So she went round to his right side, carrying the rope, bringing his attention round to that side.

He followed her with his deep brown, intelligent eyes. As she tightened the rope and raised it, he seemed to understand. With his back legs he shifted his weight the way Kirstie intended. He kept his left front leg straight and bent his right leg under him.

'That's great. Good boy!' Kirstie held her breath. If he could get up, if he could be on his feet by the time Charlie came back, she reckoned he stood a chance.

The stallion fought to keep his balance. He was pushing with the sound front leg, but it was a lop-sided movement that he'd never made before. He felt the halter rope tug his weight to one side, whinnied with pain as for a moment he tried to bend the strapped and injured knee.

The horses in the gulley heard the cry and broke apart, trotting wildly in different directions down the length of the canyon.

'Try again!' Kirstie whispered to the horse, pulling hard on the halter rope.

He pushed. His back feet found the ground, his legs straightened and he tipped forward on to the sound right knee. Kirstie pulled on the rope. Up, up!

And he made it at last, whinnying at the pain in his left knee, swaying as he rose, until he was up on his feet, towering over Kirstie, straining at the rope and pulling away from her.

'Easy, easy!' She tried to hang on. But once more the horse was powerful. Yes, he stumbled when he tried to put weight on the injured leg, but he was fighting her now, wrenching the rope from her hands. It burned her palms as he tugged free.

She gasped and let go. The horse had trusted her only so far. Now he was up and wild again, snaking the halter rope through the air in an effort to rid himself of the hated headcollar.

And the herd was gathering, waiting by the main rock fall to see what their leader would do.

Over their heads, along the ridge from the direction of the ranch, more horses were approaching. As the stallion stumbled off to join

41

his herd, trailing the rope, Lucky trotted up to Kirstie to let her know that help was arriving.

But the sound unnerved the wild horses even more. Hooves thundered along Miners' Ridge at a gallop, and they were trapped with a wounded leader in a canyon from which there seemed no escape. As Charlie and Hadley Crane appeared at the head of the gulley, the herd reared and wheeled in frantic efforts to find a way out.

'Kirstie!' Charlie raced along the edge of the canyon yelling her name. He stopped Moose and leaped from his back, coming to the edge of the cliff face. 'Your mom's not back from Denver, but Hadley here called her on the phone.'

The older man dismounted more slowly and joined him. 'She says to get you out of there!' he called, crouching alongside Charlie. His grey stetson was pulled well down over his weather-beaten face, and he was dressed in fringed leather chaps that covered the fronts of his legs, over his jeans. In spite of the recent storm, he wasn't wearing anything more waterproof than a battered denim jacket.

'But what about the stallion?' Kirstie cried.

Hadley's gaze followed the crazed path of the wild herd up and down the canyon. He saw the wounded leader limping to the far end, trailing the rope that Kirstie had attached. 'Your mom's trying to get in touch with Glen Woodford in San Luis,' he told her. 'She'll tell him the problem, then he can deal with it. But she said not to take no for an answer; she wants me to get you home!'

Kirstie groaned. Glen Woodford was the nearest vet, but it sounded like he might be out on another job. 'I don't want to leave the stallion!' she protested, tilting her head back and cupping her hands around her mouth so that Charlie and Hadley could hear.

'I got my orders!' Hadley hollered back. He began to look round the steep cliffs for a possible way out for Kirstie. 'Ain't nothing you can do about the injured horse.'

'Looks like you did plenty already!' Charlie added. He'd spotted the pale bandage around the stallion's leg. 'You got him up on his feet, didn't you?'

'But he needs me here!' Kirstie stepped quickly to one side as a grey mare split off from the herd and thundered down the canyon towards her. A distant rumble of thunder had spooked her and sent her on a crazy sprint.

'Listen, if you don't do as your mom says, I got orders to come down there and fetch you out!' The old ranch hand's gravelly voice reached her over the thudding hooves. 'You gotta climb out right now, and Charlie and me will get you back to Half-Moon Ranch before the boss arrives!'

'What about Lucky?' Leaving the wild horses trapped here was one thing, but she couldn't ever think of going home without her palomino.

There was silence as the two men scanned the cliffs.

'You could try leading him out!' Charlie yelled. 'There ain't a track no more, but Lucky's smart. He can help you find a way up to the ridge!'

More horses thudded by, churning up mud and splattering it over Kirstie's already soaked jeans and T-shirt.

'Yep, try that,' Hadley agreed. 'Don't ride him, though. It ain't safe.'

Kirstie pushed her hair back from her forehead and glanced at the stallion. 'He needs a suture in the gash on his leg!' she told them. 'Maybe his knee's even broken; I can't say.'

'Leave that to Glen!' Hadley grew impatient. 'Anyhow, if it's that bad, there ain't no point losing sleep wondering how to get him out, is there?'

She knew that the old wrangler was saying in so many words that a horse with a broken knee would have to be shot. Her heart thumped against her ribcage and she couldn't answer.

'Are you coming up or are we coming down?' Charlie demanded, standing hands on hips at the edge of the cliff.

There was nothing else for it; she and Lucky would have to abandon the wild horses to their fate until the vet from San Luis arrived. In any case, Glen Woodford would probably call at the ranch before coming up to Dead Man's Canyon, so Kirstie calculated that the best thing to do would be to be there to explain. 'We're coming!' she yelled, taking the palomino's reins and looking for any likely path to climb.

As they trod carefully through the debris of rocks left by the landslide, and with the lightning flashing in the bruised blue sky over distant Eagle's

Peak, she kept one eye on the stallion. He was still on his feet, but his head was down, his left leg lifted off the ground. Then he shook his head from side to side, making the halter rope flail through the air.

'Wait here,' she told Lucky, making another quick decision. Then she shouted up to Charlie and Hadley. 'He hates the headcollar; I want to take it off before we leave.'

'You sure?' Charlie queried.

'Yep. I promised.' 'Not for long' was what she'd told the horse. Even if it helped the vet when he eventually got here for her to leave the collar on, how could she break her word and leave the rope swinging from the hated harness?

So she dropped Lucky's reins and moved in quickly on the stallion, almost before he was aware. The rest of the herd beat a retreat, and she was able to catch hold of the rope, ease in, unbuckle the strap and slip his head out of the collar in one swift move. The black horse reared away, then stumbled on to his injured leg. But she'd freed him according to her promise. He limped away and joined the herd.

'Get a move on, Kirstie!' Hadley insisted. He pointed down at Lucky. 'Your horse is showing you how!'

Sure enough, Lucky had set off by himself up the steep, rocky slope. Surefooted as ever, he eased himself over boulders, testing for loose stones and taking a sensible route towards where the two men stood.

Kirstie scrambled after him. For the first time since Ronnie Vernon's reckless race out of the canyon on Silver Flash, she realised how tired she was. Her legs felt heavy and stiff, her cut hands began to throb as she hauled her way up the steep slope.

Half way up, Lucky stopped to wait in the thin drizzle that was still falling. Kirstie caught him up.

'You OK?' Hadley checked.

She looked up and nodded.

'Just follow the horse,' the old man insisted.

On they went. Sometimes Lucky would misjudge his footing and a stone would break loose and fall. Sometimes it would be Kirstie stretching for a handhold that held them up.

'Don't look down!' Charlie hissed as she neared

the top of the ridge. He caught hold of Lucky's reins as the horse finally made it. Handing them to Hadley, he reached down again to haul Kirstie up the final stretch.

'Don't worry, I won't!' She knew about the dizzying drop into the canyon without having to look. She was glad for the strength of Charlie's arm as he lifted her to safety.

And then she did turn and gaze back the way they'd come. With Lucky breathing hard beside her, and Hadley hurrying them along, she paused.

'What do you think? Is his leg broken?' she murmured to Charlie, who was staring down at the herd of wild horses, taking one last look.

The young wrangler shrugged. 'Best leave that to Glen Woodford.'

'I hope it's not.' She watched the stallion limp to the far end of the canyon surrounded by his herd. He was moving around; that was good. But he was bending down to nip at the makeshift bandage, trying to scratch and bite at it. It looked like it wouldn't be long before he managed it, then perhaps the bleeding would start afresh. Kirstie sighed helplessly.

'Let's go,' Hadley insisted, already astride his horse and handing Kirstie her reins.

Kirstie mounted Lucky. A numbness threatened to set in the moment the horses began to move away along the ridge, but she fought it off. She had to stay clear-headed to explain to people back at the ranch exactly what had happened. Glancing up, she saw that the rain clouds over the far-off mountain still hadn't cleared.

So she turned in the saddle to catch a last glimpse of the black stallion. He looked up at the departing figures on Miners' Ridge. 'We'll be back,' she promised.

Her voice was lost in a dull roll of thunder, her face pale and drained under the latest flash of forked lightning in the stormy sky.

4

'I know how much you care about this injured horse, but you don't go anywhere or do anything until you've changed your wet clothes,' Sandy Scott told Kirstie.

'But, Mom . . .'

'No buts.'

'But . . .'

Sandy grabbed her by the shoulders and turned her to face the stairs. 'Scoot! Go on up and find some dry things!'

Kirstie felt herself shunted upstairs. Matt gave her a grin in passing, and flung a towel at her. The grin said, 'Better do as she says!'

As she got rid of Kirstie, Sandy spread her hands in a gesture of helplessness. 'I turn my back for a single morning, and what happens?'

'You can't blame the kid for a landslide!' Matt protested. 'Even Kirstie couldn't stop a mountain collapsing on her!'

'But if there's trouble around, she'll find it.' Sandy didn't bother to lower her voice as she got busy in the big ranch-house kitchen, putting coffee on the stove and finding mugs for Charlie and Hadley. 'How come it was Kirstie who went up Dead Man's Canyon ahead of the rest?'

'That was down to me,' Charlie admitted, his own voice quiet and subdued. 'I had a small problem down the line.'

'It wasn't Charlie's fault!' Kirstie yelled from her bedroom. She pulled open drawers and turfed out dry shirts until she found the one she wanted. She changed, then gave her fair hair a rapid rub with the towel. Where in the world was Glen Woodford? She'd arrived at the ranch after half an hour's weary ride to find her mom and brother, but no sign of the vet.

In double-quick time she was changed and taking the stairs two at a time to join the others.

'These wild horses; where do you reckon they came from?' Sandy was asking Hadley Crane.

The wiry old man shrugged. 'I did hear tell of a herd up by Eden Lake a week back.' His slow voice drawled over every word. He was standing, hat in hand, with his back to the wood-burning stove. His jacket steamed, his leather chaps were still tied firmly round his long legs.

'And these are the same ones?'

'Could be. From what I heard, no one got close enough to take a proper look.'

Kirstie listened hard. She knew that Eden Lake was way up above 10,000 feet. The winter snow would still be on the ground, lying in the rock crevices and covering the mountain tops. The meadows between the peaks would only just be beginning to show green. It made sense that if the wild herd had been spotted up there, they would since have moved down the mountains for better grazing.

As she figured it out she felt her brother, Matt, sidle up to her. 'Watch out; one lecture coming up,' he warned.

'From Mom?'

Matt nodded. 'She was real worried.'

'I was OK. It was the black stallion I was thinking about.'

'Yeah!' he grinned. 'So tell me something new!'

Kirstie blushed as Matt teased her about her obsession. 'What would *you* have done? Found him under a pile of rocks and just left him?'

'Nope. I'd have done about the same as you, I guess.'

This time she grinned back. She and Matt didn't look alike; he was tall and dark, where she was middle-sized and fair. He had light hazel eyes like their dad, hers were soft grey like her mom's. Everyone said Matt was good-looking, the image of his absent father. 'Beautiful but dumb,' their mother would joke with a touch of regret.

But even though they looked different, Kirstie knew that her brother shared her love of horses.

'So how's the stallion?' he asked her now. All he'd heard so far was a garbled story told in snatches by Charlie as Matt had helped him unsaddle the horses in the corral.

'Lost a lot of blood,' Kirstie reported. 'The cut on his knee's real bad and real dirty. I guess he needs a tetanus shot and antibiotics.'

'Charlie thinks maybe his leg's broken?' Matt said quietly, as their mom went on to discuss with Hadley the chances of shifting the pile of rocks that blocked the entrance to Dead Man's Canyon.

Kirstie shrugged and turned away. Only Glen Woodford would be able to tell them that. For now, all they could do was wait. And for Kirstie, waiting was hard.

'That's a mighty big landslide back there.' Hadley scratched his head where the hair grew short and iron-grey. 'I reckon it'll take some serious earth-moving equipment to pull that pile of rocks away.'

Charlie nodded. 'It's the only way to get the stallion out of there,' he reminded them. 'No way can he do what Lucky did and climb out by himself.'

Sandy Scott chewed her lip as she thought it through. Dressed in shirt and jeans like the men on the ranch, but slight and feminine under her workmanlike clothes, she wore her fair hair pulled loosely back. Her young-looking face was tanned from working in the clear summer sun, but it was creased right now by a worried frown. 'The problem is, we still have a ranch to run,' she reminded them. 'Finding equipment to move the rocks and rescue this horse sounds like it's gonna take a whole lot of time.'

This was where Matt stepped in. 'Let me take over from Hadley and lead one of the rides this afternoon,' he suggested. 'That leaves one man free to go back to Dead Man's Canyon.'

Hadley grunted, then nodded. 'I reckon I could get over to Lennie Goodman's place at Lone Elm and borrow his JCB. If I get the go ahead, I could drive the machine along Meltwater Trail and start work.'

'Let me come!' Kirstie joined in. Lone Elm was a trailer park a couple of miles along the creek. The owner, Lennie Goodman, used the big yellow tractor-type vehicle with a giant metal scoop across the front to shift earth and make new sites for the big trailers and recreational vehicles that visited the area.

Sandy glanced at her watch. 'The guests are over in the dining-room having lunch. We have half an hour before the afternoon rides. If we all lend a hand to saddle up the horses, I reckon Hadley and Kirstie could take the afternoon off.'

'Great!' Kirstie jumped in, taking her mom at her word. She headed for the door, jamming a baseball-cap on to her head, urging Hadley to hurry.

But the old man never did anything in a rush. He said he would ring Lennie Goodman to check things out, sending Charlie after Kirstie across to the corral to help prepare the horses for the afternoon ride. Soon Matt and Sandy joined them there too.

Kirstie went from horse to horse along the tethered row. She checked their stirrups and tightened their cinches after Charlie and Matt had lifted the heavy saddles across their broad backs. When she came to Silver Flash, however, she saw that the big sorrel horse stood in his headcollar, without saddle or bridle.

'Ronnie Vernon won't be riding this afternoon,' Charlie told her. 'He says he wants to go fishing instead.'

'Hmm.' She wrinkled her nose, then sniffed. Personally, after the way he'd disobeyed orders and raced Silver Flash up out of the canyon this morning, she wouldn't care if the man never rode again.

'He feels pretty bad,' Charlie reported.

'Tell me about it.' She raised her fair eyebrows until they disappeared under the peak of her cap. A glance towards the dining-room showed her the man himself walking quickly in the other direction, away from the corral. 'You could say he was the reason the stallion got hurt.'

'You mean he started the landslide?' Matt frowned.

Sandy stopped work to listen.

Kirstie untethered Silver Flash, ready to lead him out to the ramuda, the strip of grassland by Five Mile Creek. 'He's the one who set the first rocks sliding by making his horse lope up the track.'

'Yeah, but there was a lot of rain coming down that ridge.' Charlie stepped in to remind them that Vernon shouldn't take all the blame. 'The water loosened the whole thing up. It could've happened to anyone.'

Sandy nodded, giving Kirstie a meaningful look. 'Let's leave it, OK?'

Kirstie blushed, realising that she might be being hot-headed. She was worked up by vivid memories of the injured horse. 'Sorry,' she said quietly.

'No, it's OK, I understand.' Her mom walked alongside as Kirstie led Silver Flash down to the meadow. 'They tell me you fixed the stallion up pretty good.'

'Let's hope.' She recalled her last view of him, angered by the bandage around his leg, trapped in the canyon as more rain clouds rolled down the mountain.

'You did a good job, Kirstie.' Sandy watched her daughter put Silver Flash to graze, then stretched an arm around her shoulder.

'I wish Glen Woodford would get here!' Try as she might, she couldn't get the main problem out of her mind: the first-aid treatment she'd given the badly injured horse wouldn't hold out for long. What the stallion really needed was a vet. And quick.

But she was distracted by the sight of a new figure riding on a bike down the dirt track from the main gates of Half-Moon Ranch. She recognised the short red hair and long limbs of her best friend, Lisa Goodman. Lisa was Lennie Goodman's grand-daughter, the same age as Kirstie and in the same grade at San Luis Middle School.

'Hey!' Lisa spotted Kirstie and Sandy and veered across the grass towards them. 'I was at Lone Elm when Hadley called!' she explained, flinging her bike down. 'He told us what happened.'

'Can your grandpa lend Hadley the earth-mover?' Kirstie asked.

'Sure. He's driving it over from the trailer park right now. I came on ahead.' Breathless from her ride, Lisa walked back to the corral with Kirstie and her mother. 'Sounds like you got a real problem on your hands,' she gasped. 'Can I come see?'

Quickly Kirstie nodded. She knew Lisa wouldn't be in the way. 'Hadley can take over and drive the JCB when your grandpa brings it. We'll saddle Cadillac for you . . .'

'Best ask Matt first,' Sandy reminded them. 'He's back home now, remember!'

'Ask me what?' Matt came out of the tack-room to catch the end of the sentence. He'd taken off his college clothes and wore his stetson and riding-boots instead, ready for the afternoon's work. 'Does someone want to borrow my horse by any chance?'

They arranged with him for Lisa to ride Matt's white gelding, and while they were doing this, a black Jeep rode down the track to the ranch house.

'Glen Woodford!' Kirstie cried, breaking away from the group. She climbed the corral fence and ran to meet him. 'What kept you?'

Ignoring her question, the vet jumped down from the Jeep, slammed the door and strode towards her. 'Hey, Kirstie, I hear you can put me in the picture. How's this injured horse of yours doing?'

As she explained, Charlie went out to the ramuda to fetch yet another horse, this time for the vet. The wrangler said they should ride across country to the canyon to save time. 'Dirt roads round here are flooded,' he told them. 'According to Lennie, Five Mile Creek broke its banks.'

Glen nodded and went to fetch his bag from the

car, while Kirstie ran for a saddle-bag for him and strapped it on to the back of his horse's saddle. Meanwhile, Lisa was up on Cadillac, ready and waiting.

'You got a two-way radio with you?' Sandy asked, as Kirstie mounted Lucky.

She nodded.

'Keep us in touch. I'll be out leading the beginners' ride.' Sandy glanced round to see the first guests leaving the dining-room and heading for the corral.

Glen Woodford promised to keep an eye on both girls. 'We should reach the canyon before Hadley gets there with the JCB,' he guessed. 'According to Kirstie, I should be able to climb down from the ridge. If it goes well, I can treat the horse's injuries, give him a couple of shots of Procaine, and be out of there before the work on moving the rocks begins. Then it'll be up to Hadley to make a way out for the whole herd.'

'Let's go!' Impatient to set off, her hopes raised by the vet's confident words, Kirstie tapped her heels against Lucky's sides.

The willing palomino strode out across the

corral, followed by Lisa on Cadillac and Glen on a brown and white six-year-old paint called Yukon.

'Forget the trails!' Kirstie called over her shoulder, heading Lucky straight up the slope behind the ranch. 'We'll bushwhack across country; it'll be quicker!' She calculated roughly forty-five minutes to the canyon, caught a glimpse of the giant yellow earth-mover trundling slowly along Meltwater Trail as they rose high through the aspen trees. Overhead, the clouds still threatened, but for the moment the rain held off.

Three-quarters of an hour of pushing the horses uphill, picking their way clear of the lime-green aspens into the darker, spikier ponderosa pines. Silent except for the occasional snorting of the hardworking horses, the three riders concentrated on finding the quickest route to Miners' Ridge.

'What's this Procaine shot you mentioned earlier?' Lisa asked Glen as they climbed the final slopes. Though she lived at a diner in town with her mother, Bonnie Goodman, and didn't ride as often as Kirstie, she'd kept up well.

'Procaine is a type of Penicillin,' the vet explained. 'And the stallion will need one big dose of tetanus, since these are wild horses we're dealing with and there's no chance of them being immunized already.'

'And will you stitch the wound?' Lisa quizzed.

Glen shrugged. 'Don't know yet. Sutures don't generally hold if the laceration is across a joint. I may be able to give him something to keep down the swelling; let's hold on and see what we find when we get there.'

Kirstie listened without breaking her own silence. The other two were talking as if the stallion's leg wasn't broken, she realised. She hoped they were right.

She let Lucky pick his way up the steep hill, ducking to avoid branches, keeping her weight slightly forwards in the saddle. Soon they would reach the ridge. Noticing Lucky's ears prick forward to listen, she motioned for Glen and Lisa to keep quiet.

'Are we almost there?' Lisa called after a minute or two of now silent progress.

Kirstie nodded. They were coming to mounds of waste stone, long since grassed over; stony relics left by the goldminers way back last century. They would dig deep into the mountain with dynamite and picks, haul the rock out to the mine entrance and dump it before burrowing back deep into the earth. During one bad winter a big explosion had killed many miners, and the accident had given the nearby deep gulley its name. Beyond the rough mounds the long, narrow ridge that overlooked the canyon began.

'That's weird.' Kirstie tilted her head to one side. Like Lucky, she'd been listening hard. 'I can't hear anything.'

Glen Woodford rode up alongside. 'So? What should we hear?'

'Hooves,' she explained. Earlier that morning, the wild horses had made a lot of noise as they pounded up and down the canyon. Now all was silent. 'Really weird!'

'Maybe they're resting.' Lisa looked for an explanation. 'Or listening to us sneaking up on them.'

They rode on until they reached the top of the ridge and were able to look down.

Still no noise. No restless shifting of hooves, no nervous whinnies echoing from the cliffs. Nothing.

'Empty!' Kirstie gasped.

No mares and foals huddled together, jostling down the far end of the gulley.

'How come?' Lisa stared at the blocked entrance where the fallen rocks towered, seemingly too high for a horse to climb.

Kirstie slipped from the saddle and crouched by the sheer drop. 'I don't know!' she breathed. Her hands gripped at the edge of the cliff as she peered down.

The canyon was deserted. There wasn't a living thing down there. But how could a whole herd of wild horses have escaped? And the biggest question of all; where in the world was the injured black stallion?

5

'Where in the world?' was a good question. This out-of-the way place with its unhappy history and its recent sudden disaster was starting to feel like it wasn't in the real world after all. Maybe Kirstie had got it wrong, had imagined the storm and the landslide, the black stallion and the wild herd; maybe she'd dreamed them all.

'Weird!' Lisa echoed Kirstie's uneasy doubts.

Glen Woodford got down slowly from Yukon, pausing to unstrap the saddle-bag and bring his vet's kit with him. He came and crouched at the edge of the ravine beside Kirstie and Lisa, hunching his broad shoulders inside his dark green jacket. 'What do we reckon?' he asked, calm as ever.

Kirstie shook her head. 'They were here!' she insisted. 'And there was no way out!'

Lisa stood up and walked a few steps along the ridge to peer down the canyon from a different angle. 'Zilch,' she reported in a flat voice. 'Big round zero.'

'OK, you guys, let's get this clear.' The vet looked Kirstie straight in the eyes. His square, even-featured face beneath the neat dark hair was serious but showed no sign of irritation. 'This is the right place?'

This time Kirstie nodded. 'For sure. You can ask Charlie.' No way could she have mistaken the canyon.

Glen considered things. 'So maybe the herd climbed out after you left.'

'Maybe.' She was prepared to admit it was possible. 'If they watched Lucky and me pick a new way up to the ridge, I guess they could have got the idea and followed.'

She pictured the dozen or so horses tackling the difficult route.

'But there were foals?' Glen asked. 'The mares would have a tough time leading them up the cliff.'

'I know.' Kirstie sighed and appealed to Lisa for a bright idea.

Lisa looked sideways out of her green eyes, then turned away, muttering.

'Well, maybe. But what beats me is how this injured stallion made it out.' The vet stood up and gazed around, as if the answer to the mystery might be across the far side of the canyon, or further up the mountain. 'You say the leg was real bad?'

'OK, listen. Number one, he was knocked unconscious by falling rocks. Number two, he lost a lot of blood.' Kirstie grew desperate to convince them. 'That means he would be weak. And number three, the knee was so bad I thought it might even be broken!'

Glen took this in. 'So the good news is, you were wrong.' He went on in response to her blank look. 'The knee wasn't that bad . . . not broken, so he found he could put his weight on it and follow the other horses up the track.'

'In other words, he made it out of there on his own?' Lisa got the idea. 'Which means he's doing OK.'

Taking a deep breath, Kirstie nodded slowly. 'I guess.'

'What else?' The vet invited any other explanation. '. . . Which means he didn't need my help after all,' he said after a long pause.

Kirstie felt her face grow hot and flushed at the idea that she'd dragged Glen Woodford all the way from San Luis under false pretences. 'I'm real sorry,' she stammered.

'Don't be.' He smiled kindly, returning to Yukon to pack his vet's kit back into the saddle-bags. 'This kind of happy ending I *like*!'

'So, what we do now is radio a message through to your mom with the good news, then get back to the ranch in time for one of your brilliant cowboy cookouts!' Lisa quickly looked on the bright side. She glanced up at the lightening sky and unzipped her yellow waterproof slicker. 'Saturday. Cookout day. What's to eat?'

'Hmm?' Reluctant to leave the ridge, Kirstie still stared down into the empty canyon. 'I got another idea,' she said slowly.

Lisa came close. 'How come I get the feeling I'm not going to like this so-called idea?' she asked, gingerly crouching down beside Kirstie.

Through her continuing worries about the stallion and her puzzled surprise at finding Dead Man's Canyon empty, Kirstie managed a grin. 'Because it doesn't involve supper at Half-Moon Ranch?' she quipped.

'What's with the "we"?' Lisa demanded as she stood by Cadillac's side and waved Glen Woodford and Yukon off down the mountain. 'You told your mom that "we" wanted to camp the night by Dead Man's Canyon!'

She made Kirstie laugh with her over-the-top expression of disgust. '*We* want to find the stallion, don't we?'

'Yeah . . .'

'And *we* like sleeping out in summer?' She'd persuaded her mom that it would be great for her and Lisa to make camp up here.

'What will you use for a tent?' Sandy had asked over the two-way radio. 'And what will you eat?'

Kirstie's answer had been that Matt could ride up to the ridge before supper with the camping gear and food for both the girls and the horses.

Sandy Scott had thought about it, then asked her to hand over the radio to Glen Woodford for his opinion.

'They'd do fine,' the vet had told her with a wink at the girls. 'No problem!'

So it had been fixed. Kirstie and Lisa were sleeping out.

A message had been sent to Hadley that the earth-moving equipment wouldn't after all be needed right away. The wrangler had turned around and begun to head back to Lone Elm trailer park. And Matt had, as expected, been easy-going about bringing supplies when Sandy had reached him by two-way radio.

'Great, Mom. Thanks!' Kirstie had clicked off the radio just as the vet had been ready to leave. Now she too waved and wished him a safe journey back to the ranch.

'So . . . ?' Lisa watched Glen disappear down the slope, then took off her slicker, rolled it and stuffed it into a saddle-bag hitched to the back of Cadillac's saddle.

'So, we wait till Matt gets here with the feed for Cadillac and Lucky. Then we pitch the tent and cook beans and burgers . . .'

'Yuck!' Lisa pulled a face.

'You said you wanted a cook-out!' Kirstie reminded her.

'Yeah. I was thinking more like chicken, marinated and grilled over an open fire. Baked potatoes, coleslaw . . . the full works. Not beans!' Lisa's face was comically disappointed.

'So . . . cowboy-up!' she told her with a big grin. It was the Scott family's motto, half-jokey, half-serious. 'It's tough, but you know we can do it!'

Lisa rolled her eyes again and pretended to sink against the rough bark of the tall pine tree. 'There you go with that "we" thing again!' she sighed.

The small, dome-shaped tent was up. Beans were cooking on the tiny stove.

'You don't find it kinda . . . spooky up here?' Matt mentioned as he gave Lucky and Cadillac their feed.

'Nope!' Kirstie said with lightning speed.

'Yep!' Lisa shot back.

'To me it feels like this place never gets the sun,' Matt went on. 'It's kind of shadowy, reminds me of, well, spooks, I guess.'

'Thanks, Matt!' Kirstie muttered. Lisa was already jittery enough, without him putting his size ten boots in it.

'Oh, don't . . .' Lisa stared around at the lengthening shadows. A breeze in the trees rattled branches. Some small creature, a chipmunk or a ground squirrel, scuttled off through the bushes.

Matt smiled to himself. He waited until Lucky had finished feeding, then let him wander off to a safe distance to chew on a small patch of new grass. 'All those dead miners,' he reminded them in a ghostly voice. 'Lost in the rush to grab gold from the mountain. Killed by greed!'

'Yeah, that was way back,' Kirstie insisted. 'You're talking centuries here.' Nevertheless, she did glance up from the stove towards the grassed-over mounds of waste from the old mines.

Lisa followed her gaze. 'What's that?' She pointed with a shaking hand about fifty metres up the hill to what looked like a cave between the mounds.

'That's an old mine entrance.' Matt saw she was hooked on his story. 'I guess it goes pretty deep; a black hole into the heart of the mountain! A scar on nature left by man's lust for gold!'

Kirstie jumped up from stirring the pan. 'Don't listen to him,' she told Lisa, striding over to Matt. 'He's winding us up.'

'Me?' His eyes were still smiling. 'Would I?'

'Yes, you would!' Kirstie turned him around and marched him back towards Moose. 'Go home, Matt!'

Swinging into the saddle, laughing out loud, he prepared to do as he was told. 'So why the camp?' he asked before he left. 'Why here? Why now?'

'Because!' Kirstie refused to answer. She stood, arms crossed, looking up at him, waiting for him to go.

'Because she wants to find the black stallion.' Lisa spelled it out. 'Because she can't believe he got out of there alone, without help. She thinks he's still around here some place, needing her.

And you know Kirstie; once she gets a notion, she just won't let go!'

'Promise me one thing,' Matt had insisted before he finally agreed to leave them alone on Miners' Ridge. 'You won't climb down the canyon looking for the horse before daylight.'

'It's a deal.' Kirstie knew he was right. Trying to find a way down was too risky in the gathering dusk. The plan was for her and Lisa to climb into their sleeping-bags the moment it grew dark, get as much sleep as they could, then get up at first light the next morning to continue the search.

'So who can sleep?' Lisa said now that Matt had finally gone. They'd finished the chores, made sure that Cadillac and Lucky were safely tethered and crawled into the tent for the night.

Kirstie was still crouched by the entrance, looking and listening. Except for the rustle of wind through branches and the occasional screech of an owl, the mountain was silent. Ignoring Lisa's question, she went on with her own train of thought. 'If you figure it out, even if the stallion did get out of the canyon somehow, there's no

75

way he can have gone far. He'd be too weak from losing so much blood . . .'

'What was that?' Hearing a new noise, Lisa dived deep into her sleeping-bag and pulled it up round her chin.

'. . . And if he's weak, maybe another stallion in the herd will take over from him as leader and guide the others some place else. That means the black stallion gets left behind. And you know there are mountain lions on Eagle's Peak . . .'

'Lions?' Lisa squeaked. Her head disappeared into the sleeping-bag so that only her curly red hair showed in the glow from the lamp which hung from the roof.

'And black bears. The bears are no problem to the stallion. But a cougar's different.' Kirstie knew that, though rare and seldom seen, a mountain lion would attack a horse weakened by injury. 'They hunt at night,' she told Lisa in a worried voice.

'Don't tell me!' Lisa pleaded.

'So you see, we need to get up at dawn and be out on the trail looking for clues.' She thought ahead, oblivious to the trembling heap inside the sleeping-bag next to her. 'Say we do pick up a track and find him. Say he's weak and all alone. We can stay with him, radio Mom at the ranch, and she can fetch Glen back to give him the shots he needs.'

'Sure,' Lisa said faintly.

Zipping up the tent, Kirstie turned and sighed. She switched off the lamp and threw the tent into complete darkness. 'See, since he didn't get those antibiotics he could be in pretty bad shape by now.' Wearily she crawled fully dressed into her own sleeping-bag. 'In fact, Lisa, I know Glen was trying to make out things looked good for our sakes, but if you really think about it, it's pretty clear to me that the horse could actually die!'

'Help! . . . Help me!'

Rocks crashed down from the roof of a dark tunnel. Dust rose. Men choked and cried out. One picked himself up from the ground and staggered away, arm raised to shield his stooped head from the falling debris.

'I can't get out! I'm trapped! Somebody, help me!'

Voices wailed in the thick blackness. Wild eyes,

anguished faces under a landslide of heavy rocks.

Kirstie beat her fists in the air. Her legs thrashed inside a confined space. 'Help!' she cried, sitting bolt upright.

'Wake up!' Lisa was shaking her. 'You're having a nightmare. Kirstie, wake up!'

She opened her eyes, made out the dome of the tent in the grey light before dawn. Her legs were trapped inside the twisted sleeping-bag, but there were no rocks, no miners suffocating in a dusty tomb. She took a deep breath and, for a few seconds, hung her head forward and buried her face between her hands.

'Are you OK?' Lisa waited until she looked up again.

Kirstie nodded. 'Sorry I woke you.'

'You didn't. I was already awake, looking out for mountain lions . . . bears . . . ghosts . . .' She gave her friend a wry grin. 'Didn't spot any, though. But wait till I see your brother!'

Shaking off the nightmare and reaching out to unzip the tent for fresh air, Kirstie spied Lucky and Cadillac standing quietly under the nearby trees. Both horses looked pale and unreal in the morning mist as they stretched their tethers to turn their heads at the sound of the zip.

She crawled out on all-fours, feeling the cold dew on the grass. Lifting her hands to her hot face, she cooled herself down.

'You're sure you're OK?' Lisa followed her out, already dressed in shirt and trousers.

'Yep. Glad to be awake,' Kirstie confessed. Sleeping out was usually more fun than this, with a saddle-bag full of potato chips and Hershey bars for breakfast, and sun breaking through the trees. Today there was no sun; just more clouds and the wet mist clinging to the ridge. From somewhere deep in the canyon, she recognised the sound of a bobcat's yowl.

Cadillac skittered sideways at the noise. He knocked into Lucky, who tossed his head and pulled at his tether.

With her stomach still churning from the nightmare, Kirstie stood up. Down below, lost in the mist, the bobcat went on making his high-pitched racket. 'I wonder what got into him?'

'And the horses.' Lisa glanced nervously towards Dead Man's Canyon, then over at Lucky and

Cadillac. 'You know something? I'm not the only one who doesn't like this place.'

'I agree. What do you say we saddle up and get out of here fast?' Kirstie suggested, eager in any case to begin the search for the black stallion.

She was heading towards Lucky when a grey shape came hurtling out of the canyon and along the ridge. About a metre long from head to the tip of its stubby tail, with a mottled coat, there was no mistaking the sturdy bobcat. He flew towards Kirstie, saw her and veered off for the trees where the horses were tied up.

It all happened in seconds; the bobcat flashing by, Cadillac smelling and hearing him before he saw him, the wrench at the halter rope, the brittle branch snapping.

'Watch out!' Lisa yelled a warning, too late.

The branch which tethered the two horses had broken. Cadillac reared, dragging Lucky off-balance. The branch cracked and splintered, fell apart, leaving the startled horses free to gallop.

Kirstie stood by, helpless, as the bobcat swerved, then darted between Lucky and Cadillac. Their flailing hooves crashed down inches from where he ran. Then he was clear, darting through the trees out of sight.

'Easy!' Kirstie cried.

Cadillac reared again. A fragment of branch swung from the end of his rope. It crashed against Lucky and sent the palomino prancing towards the edge of the canyon. From higher up the hill, the bobcat gave out his eerie yowl.

Twisting and rearing, sliding and kicking in their efforts to free themselves from the dangling ropes, Cadillac and Lucky ignored Kirstie's call. The mist swirled around them as they struggled. It disguised the sheer drop into the canyon, swallowed first Cadillac's pale, bucking shape, then Lucky's.

Rooted to the spot, Kirstie and Lisa heard a shower of loose stones rattle over the edge of the cliff. The sound of metal shoes on granite rang out.

Then Lucky whinnied, and the sound seemed to unlock Kirstie from her frozen position midway between tent and trees. She jerked into action, sprinting for the cliff, praying she and Lisa would be able to guide Lucky and Cadillac away from the lethal edge.

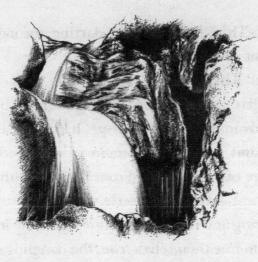

6

'It's OK, Kirstie, I've got Lucky!' Lisa was there before her. She'd seized the palomino's halter rope and held tight, as Kirstie ran through the wet mist.

Kirstie saw a dim outline. Lucky tossed his head and reared, only a few metres from the cliff. When he came down, he ducked, then kicked out with his hind legs, narrowly missing Cadillac behind him. The white horse skewed sideways, away from the edge.

'Easy, Lucky, easy!' Lisa got things under control.

She steadied the frightened horse, leaned into him and pushed him out of danger while Kirstie changed direction and went after Cadillac, disappearing once more into the mist.

'Steady.' She found the big horse standing by one of the mossed-over mounds of waste from the old mine and approached carefully, speaking in a low voice. 'The bobcat's gone. Nothing to be scared about any more.' Privately, Kirstie wasn't so sure. She wondered what had upset the cat in the first place and sent him scooting from the canyon.

'Have you got him?' Lisa called anxiously.

Cadillac had come to a halt at a distance of four or five metres. He eyed Kirstie warily, nostrils flared, one hoof pawing the ground. 'Good boy.' Realising that the horse might bolt again at the least thing, she, too, stopped.

'Kirstie?' Lisa called again.

'Give me a couple of minutes.' She waited until Cadillac had stopped striking his foot against the ground and had lowered his head; a signal that he was ready to be approached. Then she went slowly, smoothly, towards him, softly clicking her tongue and offering him the back of her hand to sniff at.

Only when he'd leaned forward to nudge at her hand with his soft grey muzzle did she reach out to take hold of the dangling halter rope.

'OK, got him!' she called to Lisa, breathing a sigh of relief.

Cadillac snorted. Through the mist Lucky whinnied back. Then both horses agreed to be led to the spot where the tent was pitched. Soon they were safely tethered once more.

'Lousy start to the day,' Lisa murmured, as Kirstie got busy with Lucky's tack.

Kirstie nodded. 'I wish I knew what spooked that bobcat.' Taking a saddle from the low branch of a nearby tree where they'd kept it overnight, she slung it over the palomino's broad back. Smoothly she brought the cinch strap under his belly and buckled it in place.

'I'll pack the tent.' More eager than ever to be out of there, Lisa slid the flexible rods out of their casings and collapsed the dome. Quickly she rolled up the lightweight fabric, only stopping to shake off the worst of the water drops. 'It's not that I let Matt's stuff about ghosts get to me,' she insisted. 'This place would've given me the creeps in any case. I mean, look at the horses; even *they* hate being here.'

'Looks that way.' Kirstie worked on, lost in thought, listening carefully to the sounds of streams full to the brim and rushing between rocks, over ledges. Water gushed and drowned out the other noises she might have heard: of the stealthy bobcat still circling the area, or maybe fox or coyote creeping through the undergrowth.

'So?' Lisa asked, when, a few minutes later, they were packed and mounted.

Kirstie took a deep breath, glancing up at the grey sky and round at the shadowy shapes of trees and hillocks. 'So I guess we should go down.'

'Down?' Lisa groaned. 'Into Dead Man's Canyon?'

She nodded. 'Something's down there, otherwise the bobcat wouldn't have acted the way he did. But you and Cadillac could stay here.' Kirstie glanced at the friendship-bracelet on her brown wrist; a gift from Lisa earlier that spring. She held her breath for the reply.

'No way. If you go, we go, don't we, Cadillac?'

Lisa read her mind. She held up her own matching bracelet.

'Not if you don't want to. Lucky and I can do this.'

In spite of everything, Lisa grinned. 'Liar, Kirstie Scott. You *need* me to come. You know you do!'

'OK, OK.' Kirstie realised that this was what was great about Lisa. She could be scared, but she would still go ahead and join in. 'Let's you and me cowboy up together!' she decided at last.

'There's even more water coming down here than yesterday!' Kirstie had dismounted now and was leading Lucky step by step down the track. Halfway along, she paused. It seemed that every ledge was now a waterfall and every jagged surface treacherously slippy.

'It's coming down from the high peaks,' Lisa pointed out. She and Cadillac had stopped a few paces behind. The mist clung to Lisa's dark red curls so that they stuck damply to her face. Wet from head to foot, her boots squelched water. 'You know, the storm hit pretty hard yesterday. That's why the streams are so full.'

'I guess.' Kirstie went on, letting Lucky pick the safest way. 'That's why, the more I think it through, I can't believe Glen Woodford when he said the stallion could've made it out of the canyon. Like, how, when there's all this water?'

Frowning, Lisa followed. 'You mean, it's hard enough when the ground's dry? But when it's wet, it's impossible?' She seemed to agree, then thought back to the previous day. 'But hey, how come there wasn't a single horse down there when we arrived?'

Kirstie stepped along a ledge where the water came up to the top of her boots. 'How do we know that?'

'We looked, remember! Zilch!'

'Only zilch from the ridge. I mean, how do we know for sure what we'll find when we get down?'

Lisa shivered, then pulled herself together. 'Yeah, like a whole bunch of wild horses were playing a game of hide-and-seek!'

Ignoring this, Kirstie led Lucky down a track she'd spotted which would take them all the way to the floor of the canyon. 'What we need is for this mist to clear,' she muttered.

But it still clung to the cliff and swirled into the crannies and crevices in the rocks. When they finally made it to ground level, it seemed thicker and damper than ever.

'So?' Lisa challenged again. Her voice was deadened by tall walls of rock which they could feel rather than see all around them. Stepping backwards, she blundered against a boulder and overbalanced into a deep, muddy puddle.

'Listen!' Kirstie let go of Lucky's rein, knowing that there was nowhere for him to bolt even if he had a mind to. The exit from the canyon was still blocked by the landslide, and the opposite end narrowed to a dead-end, as she knew. 'Did you hear something?'

'Yeah . . . water!' Lisa stepped out of the puddle and squelched anew.

'Right!' Kirstie reacted as if Lisa had really put her finger on something. 'Lots of water!'

'So what's new?' Except that her boots were full of the stuff. Dirty water was bubbling through the seams and out over the tops.

'I mean, like, *really* lots! A waterfall!' By now, Kirstie was convinced. She set off along the rock-strewn ground towards the narrow gulley at the top of the canyon. 'A new waterfall. Like, one where there wasn't one yesterday!'

'OK,' Lisa sighed. She took off her boots one at a time to shake out the muddy water. Then she ran to catch up. 'I believe you, but I still don't see . . .'

'Ssh!' Kirstie turned, finger to her lips, eyes wide. She'd reached the end of the canyon and come up against a sheet of water falling from a high ledge.

'Is this it?' Lisa craned her neck and stared up at the waterfall, created by several streams running together and meeting on the ledge some fifteen metres above the spot where they stood. It tumbled over fast and furious, splashing into a shallow pool at their feet.

Nodding, Kirstie walked up to the edge of the pool. She felt the spray on her face, noticed a lower ledge behind the fall which was almost dry because of a rocky overhang. 'Why isn't this pool deeper?' she queried, still listening, looking, investigating.

Lisa too studied the spot. It was clear that many gallons of water per second were pouring down the fall, but that the pool where it landed was neither big nor deep. 'Maybe the water drains out some place?'

Kirstie edged around the pool. 'But where? This is supposed to be the spot where Dead Man's Canyon ends. It's solid rock. There's no place for the water to run out.'

'Through here.' Lisa pointed to where the surface of the pool swirled with eddies and small currents. She saw that the water was channelled away at the base of the low ledge. 'There's a kind of stream at the back of the waterfall, beside this ledge.'

Quickly Kirstie ran to join her. 'Water can't run through solid rock!' she gasped. It could vanish underground, but what Lisa was saying was that it ran away in a stream above the ground. Which meant there was a gap in the rock!

'There's a gulley!' Lisa was still one step ahead. She was down on her hands and knees, crawling on to the ledge behind the fall.

Almost deafened by the crashing water, Kirstie followed. The ledge sloped downhill and ran the width of the waterfall.

'Hey!' Suddenly Lisa stopped.

'What? What is it?' All Kirstie could see was a sheet of water to her left, a wall of rock to her right, and Lisa in front.

'The stream runs along a kind of gulley.' Lisa turned to whisper, as if she could hardly believe what she saw. 'Like a chasm. Really narrow. But I think it opens out again.'

'Let's go!' Kirstie felt her stomach tighten into a knot. A hidden entrance to a place she never suspected before!

So they crept on, behind the thundering water, until the ledge flattened out, turned to the right and led them on between a narrow, tall crevice where the stream ran away from the waterfall.

'Hey,' Lisa whispered. 'Do we really want to do this?' She was squeezing down the gulley, up to her ankles in water, feeling closed in by tall rocks.

'We do,' Kirstie insisted. The gulley and the stream behind the fall held the answers to all her questions. She felt they would soon solve the mystery of the missing black stallion. 'We really do!'

* * *

There was a green clearing at the end of the hidden gap with the stream flowing gently across. Grass grew, aspen trees clung to the rocky slopes, dripping moisture. A well-kept, living secret behind Dead Man's Canyon.

'Did you know about this place?' Lisa stood in the small meadow shaking her head. She turned on the spot, looking all around.

Kirstie saw a pale brown hawk swoop from one of the trees, across the cloudy sky. 'No way!' she breathed.

A breeze swept through the grass. The aspen leaves quivered, the hawk landed.

'Does *anyone* know about it?' Lisa's voice didn't lift above a whisper.

'Charlie doesn't. I don't know if Hadley does. Maybe my grandpa did.' Kirstie stepped into the middle of the clearing. She noticed the bright blue columbines growing in the long grass. 'He'd know all the grazing land for the cattle. I used to come on round-ups in the spring and fall, but I never came here before.'

'. . . Kirstie!' Lisa broke in. She grabbed her arm and pointed.

There was a thicket of young aspens at the far side of the clearing. The trees were clustered thickly, good camouflage for any living creature.

Kirstie saw a dark movement. At first she thought it was a shadow cast by the trees. She looked again. The shape was solid. It moved silently between the slender trunks. Then it emerged.

The black stallion stood clear of the aspens. He raised his head, alert to their presence. He stayed calm, watching them, waiting.

'Oh, hey!' Lisa breathed. It was her first view of the magnificent horse.

'He's alive!' Kirstie closed her eyes. When she opened them, the stallion had taken a couple of steps towards them. 'And he's walking much better!'

They stared at his injured leg. There was no bandage around the knee. It was as Kirstie had guessed; her improvised strips of fabric had done the job of stemming the flow of blood, but soon afterwards, the horse must have torn them away with his teeth. In any case, the wound looked clean.

'You know something . . . ?' In turn, Kirstie took

a few steps towards the horse. 'The cut is starting to heal.'

'That's fast,' Lisa admitted.

'It's almost like . . . like . . .' She was peering hard across the clearing, not wanting to go too close and scare the stallion.

'. . . Like someone's put grease around it!' Lisa whispered.

'Antiseptic cream,' Kirstie agreed. Then she shook her head. 'No way!'

'Right. No way!' Lisa stared again and again at the injured knee. 'But there is *something* on that cut!' she insisted.

'How? . . . Who?'

Lisa screwed up her mouth and thought hard. 'Hadley?'

Kirstie shook her head. 'He'd have said.' By now she was sure; the stallion's right knee had been smeared with a thick coating of white grease.

'Glen Woodford?' Lisa guessed. 'Maybe he came back without telling us.'

'Nope.' Kirstie couldn't believe this either. 'In any case, that grease doesn't look like something a vet would use.' Glen would have relied on jabs of antibiotic and tetanus, and left the wound open, with maybe a stitch or two to hold it together. 'It looks more like a remedy an old rancher might have used.'

Lisa shook her head and sighed. 'OK,' she said. 'We have someone who sneaks into Dead Man's Canyon behind our backs, who gets close enough to this wild horse to lead him behind the waterfall into this clearing that no one else knows about . . .'

Keeping her eyes fixed on the wary horse, Kirstie nodded.

'. . . Who knows about old remedies and can get the stallion to trust him so he agrees to separate from the herd and stays here safe in the meadow . . .'

'Yep.' This needed plenty of thought. Kirstie knitted her brows and kept on staring.

'That takes one pretty smart guy!' Lisa looked round the green space. 'One smart, *invisible* guy!'

It was strange but true. The person who had helped the stallion must have been here either during those first hours after the landslide when Kirstie had gone with Charlie and Hadley to the ranch for help, or during the night, while Kirstie and Lisa had slept. He'd made no noise, but perhaps it was him who had spooked the bobcat early that morning. He'd treated the stallion, left him to graze in peace, and slipped away without leaving any clues.

'But who?' Lisa voiced the question.

Kirstie glanced away and up at the soaring hawk against the grey sky. She looked down again at the quiet, watchful stallion and felt the knot of worry she'd carried since they'd entered the gulley begin to ease.

'A healer,' she said quietly. 'An expert. Someone who really knows about horses.'

7

Matt threw another log on the ranch house fire, then quizzed Kirstie and Lisa. 'How come you're so sure the horse didn't find his own way into the clearing?'

Lisa stood with her back to the fire, her hands cupped around a mug of hot chocolate. She shook her head. 'No way would the stallion make it by himself. Anyhow, who cleaned up the wound and put the grease on?'

Kirstie's brother thought hard. 'So maybe Glen

Woodford went back to the canyon?'

'No, we already thought of that.'

'OK, so how about Smiley up at Timberline?' Matt was looking for answers that made sense.

Smiley Gilpin was a Forest Guard who lived at a station that stood at 10,000 feet. It was his job to look after the trails and plantations of ponderosa pines.

Lisa turned to Kirstie to see what she thought.

Staring into the flames of the fire in the huge grate, Kirstie shrugged. Right now the answers to the mystery didn't much interest her. Instead, she was enjoying the warmth, the feeling of relief that the black stallion was going to be OK. 'Give Smiley a call,' she suggested dreamily.

So Matt went off to the phone, leaving Lisa and Kirstie to relax. They'd arrived back at Half-Moon Ranch after their night on Miners' Ridge just after ten thirty, to find that Sandy Scott had already left with a group of beginners to ride Bear Hunt Trail. Charlie had taken the more advanced riders deep into the mountains, to Eden Lake. So the girls had dismounted in the empty corral, leaving Hadley to unsaddle Lucky and Cadillac. Then they'd come into the ranch house, to a barrage of questions from Matt.

'What do you think? Was it Smiley?' Lisa asked. She too was eager to solve the mystery of the unknown horse doctor.

Kirstie smiled and shrugged.

'I don't get it.' Lisa put her empty mug down on the stone hearth and sat cross-legged on the brown-and-white patterned rug. 'One minute you'd do anything for this horse: you sleep out, you have nightmares, you practically risk your neck. Now it's like you don't even care.'

Kirstie gazed at the fire as the burning logs shifted and sent up fresh sparks. 'I'm just glad, that's all.'

'But don't you want to know who's looking out for him?'

'Kind of.' She pictured a man, or maybe even a woman, who knew how to approach a wild horse and win his trust. Someone who cared enough to lead him behind the waterfall into the hidden clearing, where he would be safe. In a few days' time the stallion would be well enough to make his way back into the canyon and up on to Miners'

Ridge, when he would no doubt rejoin the rest of his herd.

As Lisa gave an exasperated shrug, Matt came back. 'Smiley says it ain't him,' he reported. 'The clearing behind the canyon is news to him.'

'Great,' Kirstie murmured absent-mindedly.

Matt frowned. 'What's great about it?'

'Don't ask!' Lisa warned. 'She's on a different planet. But how about Hadley? Maybe he could tell us more.'

'Let's ask,' Matt agreed briskly. He strode across the room, grabbing his stetson from the table.

Lisa sprang to her feet and dragged Kirstie after her. 'Hadley's been here forever,' she reminded them. 'We need to find out what he reckons.'

The old ranch hand was storing Lucky's saddle in the tack-room next to the corral when Matt, Lisa and Kirstie went to join him. They walked up the short ramp into the dark, cluttered room lined with iron hooks to hang bridles from and wooden racks for the saddles.

'Sure, I know the place,' he replied slowly after Matt had described the hidden clearing. 'Good grazing land.'

His answer, laid-back and matter-of-fact as usual, drew Kirstie into the conversation at last. 'You knew? How come you never told us about it?'

'You never asked.' Hadley hung Lucky's bridle alongside Cadillac's on the row of hooks.

'How can we ask about something when we don't even know it exists?' Kirstie pointed out. She'd known Hadley all her life, since the days when her grandparents had run Half-Moon Ranch as a cattle ranch. He'd always been the same; easygoing, unruffled, and sometimes infuriating.

The wrangler shrugged. 'Ain't had no call to go there since the spring of '94,' he told them. 'That was the last round-up me and your grandpa rode out on. We heard a bunch of cattle had found their way in there. And your grandpa knew every blade of grass round here. We had no problem tracking them down and rounding them up for the summer.'

'So other old ranchers would know the clearing?' Matt suggested after a short pause.

Hadley nodded. 'Jim Mullins over at Lazy B, Wes Logan up at Ponderosa Pines—'

'Maybe one of them helped the stallion,' Lisa cut in.

'Don't count on it,' Hadley warned, going to the door at the sound of horses returning along the trail by Five Mile Creek. 'Busy cattle men don't take time out to rescue a wild horse. More likely to be a backwoods man, I reckon.'

'A drifter?' Matt considered the new idea.

Kirstie had followed Hadley to the door. She took in her mother's group of riders returning slowly along the trail, gazed out at the Meltwater Range rising steeply from the narrow valley, then up at the sky. She saw that the clouds that had clung to the peaks for the past two days were clearing at last. There were small patches of blue, and more to come.

'One of those guys who live in trailers up there in the mountains?' Lisa prompted Hadley for more information. 'Kind of drop-outs?'

Kirstie knew the type of loner they were talking about. The backwoods men chose a lonely life of hunting and fishing. They scraped an existence from the land, lived simply, moved on.

'Like who?' Matt asked. 'Give us some names.'

Hadley tipped his hat back on his head. 'A name ain't much use without an address,' he reminded them. 'And these guys don't stay in one place too long.'

'But I know who you mean,' Lisa said eagerly. 'Some of them come into San Luis for supplies once in a while. They call in at mom's diner.' Her mother, Bonnie Goodman, ran the most popular eating place in town. 'Yeah, I got it; there's Bob Tyson. He's an ex-rodeo rider. Then there's Art Fischer and Baxter Black; hippy types. They all live kind of rough in the forest.'

Kirstie listened and let her imagination run on. She pictured the rescuer of the black stallion as a man who had turned his back on a life that centred on cars, jobs and evenings in front of the television. He knew the woods and the mountains, had learned the old ways; maybe even the habits and healing methods of the Native American Indians. One thing was for sure; the mystery man cared about horses.

'They live rough and think rough,' Hadley warned. He strode out into the corral to greet the returning riders, heading first for Ronnie Vernon on Silver Flash. He helped Vernon to dismount as he went on talking to Lisa. 'Don't go getting ideas about looking them up.'

'Ideas about looking who up?' Sandy Scott inquired as she dismounted from her own horse. She tethered the skewbald to the nearest post.

When she heard the news about the mysterious horse doctor and the latest theory on who he might be, she quickly agreed with Hadley. 'Too risky,' she told Lisa and Kirstie. 'We don't know the first thing about those guys.'

'Except that one of them cares enough about the black stallion to climb down into Dead Man's Canyon and take care of him!' Kirstie objected. 'Except that he's done more for that horse than a lot of people I can think of!'

'How do we know that?' Sandy took off her white hat, then linked arms with her daughter. She led her out of the corral, followed by Matt and Lisa. They walked together past the tack-room towards the ranch house. 'Aren't you loping ahead a little bit here?'

'But, Mom . . .' Kirstie launched into her reasons for tracking down the healer. 'He'd be real interesting. I reckon he knows a lot about wild horses. We could learn things from him . . .'

Sandy raised her eyebrows and stared. 'Too

risky,' she repeated. 'Hadley's right.'

'But . . .'

'Listen.' Her mother stopped on the stretch of grass outside the house, one foot on the wooden deck that led to the front door. She spoke seriously to get her point across. 'You paint a pretty picture of your horse doctor, but you gotta know that's not the way it's likely to be.'

'How come?' Matt asked. He saw that his mom meant what she said.

'Well, just suppose you've hit on the right answer and Bob Tyson, say, is the guy who's taking care of the stallion. Now I don't know Tyson in person, and I've never met him, but I hear he's got a bad name in town for not paying his bills.' Sandy turned to Lisa for confirmation.

'I guess,' Lisa agreed awkwardly.

'He lives real rough, he owes hundreds of dollars at the grocery store and the gas station and the diner. And one more thing I know about Bob Tyson . . .'

'What?' Kirstie suspected that she wasn't going to like this one little bit. Her stomach turned over and began to tie up in another knot.

'He does know plenty about horses, like you said. He used to work the rodeos in San Luis and Silvertown.' Sandy paused to fling her hat on to the porch swing, sat down, then delivered the bad news. 'So what he does now when he wants to scrape together a few dollars is go up the mountain and trail a herd of wild horses. He picks out the best horse in the bunch, watches and waits until he can cut that one out. Then he'll lasso it and bring it down. Great. Now he has something to sell at the horse sale.'

'What are you saying?' Kirstie gasped. She had a strong picture in her head of her own black stallion being brought down by a snaking lasso, of him being dragged into the dust, tied down, bullied until the fight went out of him. His gleaming black coat would be covered in dirt, there would be fear in his eyes.

'Bob Tyson catches wild horses to sell on to the rodeo circuit,' Sandy repeated. She looked long and hard at Kirstie, then Lisa, then Matt. 'So I'm telling all three of you right here; you don't tangle with the Bob Tysons of this world.'

'No, ma'am,' Lisa agreed and hung her head.

Matt gave a quick nod.

'Kirstie?' Sandy prompted.

She hung her head and gave in at last. 'OK,' she breathed, turning on her heel and striding away from the house.

8

So much for Kirstie's belief in her mysterious horse healer. She spent the rest of Sunday doing chores on the ranch, helping Matt and Charlie to bring in logs for the fires and stacking them outside the guest cabins, then raking the dirt surface of the arena behind the corral. That evening Charlie and Matt were to give an exhibition of horsemanship there, and everything must be made neat and tidy.

But Kirstie felt too let down to work well. It was like riding Lucky up to Hummingbird Rock, feeling great, seeing that the world was a beautiful place, then suddenly, unexpectedly, falling off. She was down on the ground, covered in dirt, looking like an idiot. And she only had herself to blame.

She raked the arena with sullen strokes, head down, eyes fixed on the furrowed pattern she made with the rake. Trust her to believe that the black stallion's helper was someone you could trust. All that stuff about knowing nature and caring about horses turned out to be Kirstie's own imagination running away with her, making up romantic stories that turned out not to be true.

'Sorry,' Lisa had said quietly after Sandy had dropped the bombshell. 'I know how much this means to you.'

Kirstie had done her best to smile back at her friend. 'Sure. But I guess we can still hope.'

'How come?' Lisa was waiting for her grandfather, Lennie Goodman, to drive over from Lone Elm, pick up her bicycle and drive her down to her home in San Luis. 'You heard what Hadley and your mom said. No way can we take any more risks to save the stallion.'

Inwardly Kirstie had groaned. But she didn't

show how disappointed she felt, and had waved Lisa off in her grandpa's red pick-up truck without giving anything away.

It was only when she was alone in the late afternoon sun, working in the arena, making it ready for the evening show that she admitted even to herself how bad it was.

For a start, she really loved and admired that horse. Her first view of him in the canyon, proud and suspicious, neck arched, nostrils flared as he protected his herd, had done it. Then there was his courage. She remembered how he'd struggled through his bewilderment and pain to get to his feet after the landslide. And the stallion had trusted her. Hers was the first human hand ever to touch him as she buckled the halter on to help him. And he'd believed in her as she strapped the bandage around his leg to stop the bleeding.

Fiercely Kirstie raked the ground. The horse had permitted her touch, had allowed her to help him. And now a second human being, a man whose name might be Bob Tyson, or Art Fischer, or Baxter Black, had deceived him. The mystery man had found him trapped in Dead Man's Canyon, had offered false help in order to make money out of him. The Drifter had betrayed the horse's precious trust for the sake of a few dollars in a San Luis sale barn.

Unless . . . unless . . . Kirstie stopped work and held the rake frozen in mid-air. 'How dumb am I?'

'You say something?' Charlie poked his head around the tack-room door. It was his afternoon to clean the tack while the others took rides along the trails. With his shirt sleeves rolled up, the low sun made him look extra-tanned.

'Yeah . . . Nope!' Quickly she worked over the last corner of the arena and flung the rake into one corner of the barn. Then she made sure Lucky was still hitched to his post in the corral before she went running into the tack-room to fetch his saddle.

Charlie stood to one side and watched. 'Looks like you changed your mind about riding this afternoon.'

'Yep.' She'd been so dumb. Sure, her mom had said to stay away from the backwoods men. And that made sense, if they were as tough as Sandy said they were. Kirstie had agreed that she wouldn't go riding up the mountain looking for their beaten-up old trailers, trying to convince them not to sell her beautiful wild stallion to some ruthless rodeo organiser.

That had been the exact promise: 'OK, I'll stay clear of Bob Tyson.'

'And Art Fischer, and Baxter Black, and any other drifter who happens to be passing through.' Sandy Scott had made the situation absolutely plain.

And, though it had felt as bad as teeth being pulled, Kirstie had promised.

But she *hadn't* promised her mom not to go back to Dead Man's Canyon.

'Can't say I blame you.' Unsuspecting, Charlie looked up at the blue sky and offered to help her saddle Lucky. 'I'd take a ride myself if I didn't have this exhibition tonight.'

'Tell Mom I'll be back before sundown.' Her fingers felt clumsy as she rushed to fasten the cinch and pull down the stirrups. She mounted quickly and took the reins.

'Sure thing.' Charlie stood and watched her set off, then called after her. 'Hey, your mom's gonna ask me where you went!'

Kirstie reined Lucky back. 'Tell her Meltwater Trail,' she yelled, turning again and riding off into the sun without looking back.

Meltwater Trail and Dead Man's Canyon. That was how dumb she'd been! It had taken her since lunch to realise that her promise to her mom didn't cover riding back to the hidden clearing, finding the stallion and setting him free.

Now it was all she could think about as she urged Lucky into a trot and then a smooth lope up the hill.

Again and again she went over each step of the new plan, almost forgetting to duck the branches of the pine trees and guide the palomino over fallen trunks as they sped on. The black stallion would still be there in his clearing behind the waterfall. Perhaps the rest of the herd would be gathered nearby. Kirstie would dismount and leave Lucky on the ridge. She would take a headcollar and rope with her, and climb down into the canyon. Then she would crawl along the ledge into the meadow. Then . . .

Kirstie lurched forward as Lucky came to a

sudden stop. They'd covered more ground than she'd realised and reached fast-flowing Horseshoe Creek. Now they would have to wade across before they reached the canyon. Lucky had been heading for his usual crossing place when a figure standing on a rock in the middle of the stream brought him to a halt.

It was a man with a fishing-rod and canvas bag slung across his shoulder, obviously making his way down towards Five Mile Creek in the valley below. Nothing about him looked unusual or scary; he was medium height, with fair, short hair, wearing a padded jacket, jeans and boots. But Sandy's recent warning was fresh in Kirstie's mind. What if this man, whom she'd never seen before, was one of the drifters they'd been talking about? Maybe he was Baxter or Art? Or maybe even the notorious Bob Tyson?

The thought made Kirstie rein Lucky to the right and head off across country without waiting to greet the stranger. She felt her horse begin to blow as the hill grew steeper and they passed under the shadow of Hummingbird Rock, but she pushed him on until they were out of sight.

Then she slowed. The detour was heading them towards Miners' Ridge; she recognised the weird humps of grassed-over mine waste on the horizon. Knowing that the ridge would give her a good view down into the canyon, and finding that Lucky had soon got his second wind, she decided to carry on.

They came on to the ridge as the sun began to turn the sky pink. The dark pines lined up in silhouette, tall and straight. And beneath the trees stood the horses.

'Easy!' Kirstie breathed. Lucky gently slowed and stopped. The breeze lifted her hair and cooled her hot face as they stood gazing at the herd.

They seemed like dream horses, still as statues under the trees. But the breeze reached them and swayed their long tails. One sorrel stamped and turned her head towards the onlookers, then turned to gaze again into the seemingly empty canyon.

How long had they been waiting there, Kirstie wondered. Maybe hours. While shadows lengthened and the light drained from the hillsides, they'd been watching. She noticed a dappled grey mare standing apart from the rest, nearer to the sheer drop into Dead Man's Canyon, her head forward, long ears pricked. The mare ignored Kirstie and Lucky, and gave a low snicker that rippled through the quiet air and was swallowed by the deep sides of the ravine.

The still, silent horses listened for a reply.

Kirstie shook her head. The mare had signalled to the black stallion below, but there had been no answer.

Restless now, the herd broke up and began to mill around. Two foals cut away from their mothers and skittered on long, ungainly legs towards a stream that ran into a gulley at a blocked entrance to an old mine. A young, strong blue roan stallion trotted a hundred metres along the ridge, and with a flick of his tail and a toss of his head, wheeled and came back.

But the grey mare hadn't given up. Standing at the brink, she gave another high whinny.

It sent a shiver down Kirstie's spine. The mare was demanding an answer from her injured mate.

And this time it came. A loud, piercing cry broke from the depths of the canyon, echoing against the rocks, rising to where the herd had gathered. The black stallion had given his reply.

Kirstie tied Lucky to a tree branch and climbed down the difficult but by now familiar route into the canyon. She carried a rope slung crossways across her shoulder, her mind fixed on carrying out her plan to set the stallion free.

But she knew she must be quick if she hoped to crawl along the ledge behind the waterfall and into the clearing, because the light was fading. There was time to do it if everything went well. But the stallion might prove difficult to catch and lead out. In that case, she would have to leave him there for one more night and come back early tomorrow.

What she hadn't expected was to find him still in pain from his injury. But when she stood upright after her wet crawl behind the waterfall and stepped on to the grass, and discovered the stallion standing at the furthest point beside the copse of young aspens, she saw that he couldn't yet take his weight on his left leg. The knee was bent, the hoof raised from the ground.

But maybe . . . Kirstie went slowly forward.

Maybe with her help he would be able to limp across the meadow, through the narrow chasm and along the ledge to freedom.

The stallion tossed his head and whinnied loudly. He shifted awkwardly, almost collapsing on to the left leg, then backing away.

Kirstie paused. The horse was more lame than she'd thought. The knee joint was swollen, the covering of white grease over the wound beginning to turn brown and dirty. He staggered again in an effort to keep her at a distance.

It was no good then. Her plan depended on him being well enough to follow her out of the clearing and up the difficult track on to the ridge. But it would have to wait. Kirstie sighed and turned away. Then she stopped. But what if The Drifter came back for the stallion before her? The Drifter – not The Healer, not The Mystery Horse Doctor, since Kirstie's talk with her mom – might force him out of the canyon, bad leg or not. He wouldn't care if the wild horse was in pain, not if he could make money out of him at the sale barn.

But what could she do? Nothing. Except keep watch. Kirstie took a deep breath and tilted her head to the darkening sky. One thing was for sure; no one in their right mind would come along after nightfall to move the stallion. They were safe at least until morning.

Encouraged, she made up her mind to leave the horse where he was.

'Until daylight,' she told him, as if he could understand. And in a way, he did.

Her gentle voice, her soft movements seemed to calm him. He no longer tried to back away, stumbling on his injured leg, but stood quite still. Head up, mane ruffled by a warm breeze that whispered through the aspens and up the steep cliffs on to the ridge above, he watched her go.

'I must be crazy,' Lisa complained. She yawned and slumped in the saddle. 'It's the first day of my vacation and I get up before dawn!'

Kirstie grinned. 'You know what we say at Half-Moon Ranch; you just gotta . . .'

'. . . Cowboy up!' Lisa groaned. 'Yeah, yeah.'

She'd driven out to the ranch with her mother in answer to Kirstie's secretive phone call of the night before. Kirstie had asked her to ride back to

Dead Man's Canyon with her to look out for the stallion, but she'd warned her not to say anything to her mom. As far as the adults were concerned, Lisa and Kirstie had simply organised a breakfast ride to celebrate the beginning of the school vacation.

The two women had been surprised that the girls wanted to ride out so early, but they'd shrugged, seen them off on Lucky and Cadillac and settled down to an early morning cup of coffee over the ranch-house kitchen table.

'Better to be crazy than mean,' Kirstie said now, thinking all the time of how they must beat The Drifter and his plan to sell the stallion.

'Huh.' Lisa piled on the groans. 'Just don't tell anyone I did this, OK?'

Her good-tempered complaints passed the time until Miners' Ridge came into view against a clear morning sky.

'Sun's gonna be hot today,' Kirstie predicted. 'It's gonna melt the snow off the peaks and send a whole lot more water down.'

As if to prove her point, Horseshoe Creek seemed even deeper and faster than it had the night before. Lucky went down the bank and stepped sturdily in, swaying slightly as the water rose round his flanks and soaked Kirstie's jeans. She urged him on and he surged through, then they turned to wait for a reluctant Cadillac.

'C-c-cold!' Lisa gasped, as she too felt the water dash against her legs.

But by the time the girls made it to the ridge the first rays of sun had dried off their jeans and they were both feeling good about the plan to take another look at the stallion.

'Even if his leg's not good enough to come out of the clearing with us, we'll try to get near and talk to him,' Kirstie said as she dismounted and tied Lucky up. 'The more he gets to know us, the easier it's gonna be in the long run.'

'We can always come back later today and try again if need be.' Lisa had been the first off her horse and was ready to take the track down into the canyon.

'Or stay out here the whole day and keep watch,' Kirstie said. She was on the lookout for the herd, expecting to see the grey mare at their head. The fact that they weren't here on the ridge surprised her slightly.

'You can't be serious!' Lisa retorted, thinking of her stomach as usual. 'Stay here the whole day without a sack-lunch?'

She went on ahead, grumbling and kidding, but Kirstie stayed on the ridge, still looking out for the wild horses. She thought she heard the faint sound of hooves drumming down the hillside towards her, and then she caught sight of the young sorrel, quickly followed by a piebald. They galloped through the trees, kicking up dirt, swerving past boulders. 'Hey!' she said softly. These horses weren't playing a game of chase. Their flattened ears and reckless speed told her they were fleeing from an unseen pursuer.

Two young foals came next, skidding down the slope, their stick-like legs folding under them as they crashed down. They jerked back up on to their feet and ran on. Then more fully-grown horses came hard on their heels. Kirstie saw the fear running through their bodies, making them toss their heads and rear up. What was it? Who was chasing them?

'Say, what's happening?' Lisa had heard the noise and climbed back on to the ridge. She stopped and stared.

Kirstie took a step forward, then another. Here came the grey mare at the back of the herd, half-hidden by a cloud of dust. The horse ran more slowly, hindered by something that she couldn't quite make out.

'What's that around her neck?' Lisa cried. 'See; she's dragging a length of rope!'

Kirstie broke into a run. She saw it now; the rough slip-knot, the trailing rope that caught in the bushes as the horse ran.

The other wild horses had reached the ridge and galloped along its length. But the grey mare was winded. She saw the girls, slowed and wheeled away. Up on her hind legs, front hooves flailing, she whirled back the way she'd come.

But her path was blocked. There was a man scrambling down the mountain towards her; a dark figure in a black hat, the brim pulled well down. He spread his arms wide to threaten the mare, paused to unhitch another rope from his shoulder, then raised it over his head to launch a second lasso.

'Don't do that!' Kirstie yelled the first words that came into her head. She ran faster, straight at the grey horse.

Caught between them, the mare reared up.

The second rope snaked through the air. Kirstie leaped forward, jumped and caught it. The man's harsh voice swore. He jerked at the rope and heaved Kirstie off her feet.

'Let go of the damn rope!' he cried.

She hung on. Her arms felt as if they were being pulled out of their sockets as the stranger dragged her over the rough ground.

'Get out of my way!' he yelled again. 'I plan to rope that mare in, and no fool kid's gonna stop me!'

9

'Kirstie, let go of the rope!' Lisa begged.

Kirstie was cut and bruised, covered in dirt. But she'd hung on long enough to give the grey horse a chance to get away. Out of the corner of her eye she saw the mare turn on the spot and race along the ridge after the other wild horses. Her white mane and tail streamed in the wind. OK; *now* Kirstie would loosen her grip!

'Damn fool kid!' the man shouted, falling back as the tension on the rope suddenly slackened. He jerked it and began to coil it towards him.

Quickly Lisa helped Kirstie to her feet. She pointed at the scratches on her arms. 'You're bleeding!'

'I'm OK.' Breathing hard, her shoulders and hands hurting, she brushed herself down. 'No way was I gonna stand by and watch that!'

'But listen!' Lisa was pulling her urgently away from the angry man. 'You know who that is? It's Bob Tyson!'

Kirstie sniffed then breathed out rapidly, as if she'd been punched in the stomach. 'You sure?'

Lisa nodded. 'I've seen him in the diner.'

Glancing across, Kirstie took in the frowning features under the wide brim of the black hat. The man was unshaven and thickset, wearing a dark grey shirt and old jeans. The large silver buckle of his belt glinted in the light as he finished coiling his lasso and strode towards them.

'I could have roped that horse in if you hadn't gotten in the way!' he snarled at Kirstie. 'You know how long I'd been on her tail? Since sun-up. I had her real tired and cut off from the herd. And you had to mess-up!'

Kirstie drew herself up, tall as she could. Her

grey eyes flashed as she spoke. 'I'm glad.'

'Me too.' Lisa stood alongside. Together they could defy the horse rustler.

'No way does that mare belong in a sale barn!' Kirstie went on angrily. 'Her place is here on the mountain. This is where she belongs.'

'Along with the stallion,' Lisa added. She glared at Tyson to let him know they knew what he was up to.

But the man's face switched at the mention of another horse. His eyes narrowed, he became suspicious. 'Stallion?' he repeated.

'Quit pretending you don't know what I'm saying,' Lisa raced on. 'One black stallion in one hidden clearing!'

Kirstie watched Tyson's frown deepen. His eyes flicked shrewdly from Lisa to herself and back again.

'Oh, *that* black stallion,' he sneered.

'The one you're gonna take to the sale barn when his leg's good!' Lisa challenged. 'Only you'd better know, we're not gonna let you!'

'Shh!' Kirstie snatched at her friend's arm and began to pull her away. 'Let's get out of here!'

'I'm gonna take a stallion to the sale barn

when his leg's good?' Tyson echoed. He glanced thoughtfully up and down the hillside, then along Miners' Ridge. His gaze rested on the cliff edge and the steep drop into Dead Man's Canyon. 'A stallion in a hidden clearing?'

'Let's go!' Kirstie insisted.

'Quit pulling me!' Lisa protested. But she gave in when she saw the look of panic on Kirstie's face. She glanced again at Tyson's sneering features with a dawning realisation of what she'd done.

They left the drifter standing on the ridge, grinning after them. Running for their horses, they mounted and rode away. Away from the old mine entrance and the grassy mounds, away from the stream swollen by meltwater from Eagle's Peak. Away from Dead Man's Canyon and the horse in the hidden clearing.

'He didn't know!' Kirstie gasped at Lisa as they found the trail and pushed Lucky and Cadillac on in any direction as long as it was away from the horse rustler. 'I was watching his face all the time you stood up to him, and it hit me right between the eyes. That was the first Tyson ever heard of the black stallion!'

* * *

And now Lisa and Kirstie had to pray that the drifter didn't know the mountain well enough to discover the clearing behind the waterfall.

'After all, even the Forest Guard doesn't know about it,' Kirstie reminded her friend as they reached level ground and carried on along Five Mile Creek Trail. They tried to convince themselves that Tyson had no chance of finding the stallion. 'And no more does Charlie, and he's been riding these trails with the intermediates since winter.'

'Whereas this guy's a loner, a drifter. He moves on before he gets to know a place real well.' Lisa nodded hard. 'He shoots a few deer, catches a few fish . . .'

'Builds up a whole pile of debts . . .' Kirstie added.

'Sells a few horses that don't belong to him . . .'

'Until the sheriff rides him out of town.' She wished she felt as confident as they both sounded. She wished her heart would stop thumping and jumping with fear every time she pictured Tyson. Most of all, she wished she could think of a plan to deal with the new emergency.

'I don't reckon he'll ever find the way into the clearing!' Lisa insisted. 'My guess is, he'll forget what we told him about the stallion and keep on after the grey mare.'

'I guess.' Kirstie sighed. 'But you gotta admit, we've been wrong about a whole lot of things . . .' She tailed off, realising that they'd jumped to too many conclusions since yesterday, when they'd seized on the idea that it was a drifter up to no good who'd hidden the injured stallion in the clearing.

'You're right.' Lisa's face fell. 'We can't rely on Tyson not finding the stallion.'

They were silent for a while, as they rounded a bend in the creek and the scattered, single-storey log buildings of Half-Moon Ranch appeared in the distance.

'What we have to do is beat Tyson at his own game,' Kirstie decided. 'Now he knows about the horse, he's gonna find him for sure. Sooner or later.'

'Let's hope it's later.' Lisa gave Cadillac his head and let him trot for home.

Lucky too gained speed. 'So what we do is go back and get the horse out of there before Tyson shows up!' Kirstie insisted. 'Only this time, we get your grandpa to come along with his earth-moving machine.'

'Which he plans to do in any case.' Lisa told her that he'd mentioned it again on the drive to Half-Moon Ranch that morning. 'He knows he's still gotta move that heap of rocks and clear the entrance to the canyon,' she confirmed.

Encouraged, Kirstie went on. 'He bulldozes a way through the landslide while we fetch the horse from the clearing. Sure, the stallion can't climb up the cliff because of his bad leg, but walking right out of there on a level track once your grandpa's finished work; that's different. I reckon he could do that easy.'

Lisa nodded. 'It sounds a pretty good plan . . . if Grandpa agrees. And your mom too.'

If . . . if. If they beat Tyson to it. If the bulldozer could be brought across to Dead Man's Canyon in time. Urging their horses into a lope along the final stretch of flat ground, Kirstie and Lisa raced for the ranch.

* * *

'What I don't get is, if Tyson ain't the guy who's been looking after the stallion in the clearing, then who the heck is?' Matt spoke what was in everyone's thoughts. It was the one thing that still puzzled him, even as he rode out with Lisa and Kirstie, back to Miners' Ridge.

The girls had done a good job of convincing everyone that they needed to act fast if they were to save the black horse. Sandy Scott had returned from her morning ride and listened intently as they described the new developments, including the sighting of Tyson. She'd immediately called Lennie Goodman, who had agreed to drive the earth-mover straight over from the trailer park to the canyon. He'd estimated that it would take him a couple of hours to get there in the slow, heavy vehicle.

Matt had promised Sandy that he wouldn't let Kirstie and Lisa out of his sight all afternoon, and she'd finally reluctantly agreed to let them return to the ridge.

'Watch and wait until Lennie's bulldozed a way in,' she'd insisted. 'Then go get the stallion and lead him right out.'

Kirstie had stood at the kitchen door, shifting guiltily from one foot to the other. 'Got it,' she muttered.

'And don't even *think* of doing anything except that.' Her mom had been deadly serious. 'Straight into the clearing, straight out again. If his leg's strong enough, let the stallion go. No fooling around bringing him back to the ranch to keep an eye on him.'

'No way!' Kirstie had protested.

'You gotta be tough.'

'Sure.' She'd turned and crossed the deck, taken the two steps down on to the grass and run for the corral ahead of Lisa and Matt. She could dream of caring for the beautiful black horse, of brushing him until he gleamed, of giving him the best feed and watching his every move. But that would mean surrounding him with fences, penning him in. No, that would never work. The stallion needed freedom.

By the time she, Lisa and Matt were heading for the canyon, she'd squashed her dream and faced reality.

It was mid-afternoon by the time the three riders reached Miners' Ridge. The sun had scorched away the last of the clouds and now shone down from a deep blue sky. Yet more meltwater from the ice-bound peaks swelled the streams. In the distance, they heard the slow rumble of Lennie Goodman's bulldozer as it made its way along a lower trail.

'Remember, we stick together,' Matt reminded Kirstie and Lisa, picking up the girls' impatience as they reined their horses in by the cave-like entrance to the old mine. Since Lisa was riding Cadillac, he'd picked out Crazy Horse for himself; a big, ugly-beautiful pale tan horse with white socks and fair mane and tail.

Kirstie dismounted, then stared down into Dead Man's Canyon for signs of Bob Tyson's presence, but all seemed quiet. 'How about we all go down to check?'

The others agreed that there could be no harm in climbing into the canyon and making sure that the stallion was still safe in the clearing.

'Let's take the horses,' Lisa suggested. 'If Tyson's still hanging around the area, he could spot them, guess what we plan to do and beat us to it.'

Matt nodded. 'You and Lucky lead the way,' he told Kirstie.

So she went ahead on foot, leading the palomino, keeping a watch for any unusual movement or sound from below.

'Did you hear that? Like, branches moving, twigs snapping!' Lisa hissed. She and Cadillac were halfway down the track into the canyon, hard on Kirstie's heels, but she stopped dead and glanced anxiously back up at the ridge. 'I got this weird feeling someone's watching us!'

Third in line with Crazy Horse, Matt scanned the jagged overhangs. The heat of the sun made steam rise from the dark red rocks. He shook his head.

'Yes, I kind of . . . feel it!' Lisa protested. 'Like eyes are on us all the time!'

'Those miners' ghosts keep showing up.' Matt shrugged off the uneasy feeling that Lisa had created.

But Kirstie took her friend more seriously. She watched out for movement, saw sinister shapes in shadows, could almost pick out Tyson's dark hat and crouching figure. But no; when she looked hard, there was no one there. 'Come on!' she whispered. 'Let's go see the stallion!'

Pushing ahead, wading with Lucky through a new stream that came gushing over the ridge and across their path, Kirstie was suddenly overtaken by a fresh rush of anxiety. Not concentrating, the force of the clear, cold meltwater almost knocked her off her feet and made her lurch to catch hold of Lucky's saddle horn. Her horse stood steady long enough for her to pull herself upright and wade to safety.

'You OK?' Matt shouted above the sound of splashing water.

'Yep.' More determined than ever, she pressed on.

'When you get to the bottom, wait there for us!' her brother yelled.

Kirstie glanced back to see that Lisa was also having trouble crossing the stream. Matt seemed to be telling her to mount Cadillac and try riding across. But the ledge where they all stood was narrow, and the hold-up lengthened. Meanwhile, Kirstie decided to continue.

So much meltwater. Water everywhere. It dripped off every ledge, trickled into narrow streams. The small streams joined together to form wide waterfalls that bounced and crashed off the rocks all around.

But, while Lisa struggled with Cadillac halfway down the cliff, Kirstie and Lucky made it to the bottom. She looked back up to see where they'd come, and in a way she was relieved to see how difficult the route had been. Surely Bob Tyson would have found it impossible to pick out the way. Which meant that, most important of all, the stallion was still safe . . .

Impatiently Kirstie glanced at the main waterfall that hid the ledge entrance to the clearing. She frowned at the torrent of water that crashed into the pool at the foot of the fall. Surely the pool hadn't been that deep before? And surely the waterfall hadn't completely hidden the ledge!

Suddenly she realised what was happening. The floodwater from the melting mountain glaciers, combined with the rain from the weekend storms, would soon make it impossible to use the entrance. The water would rise faster and faster as the sun continued to melt the snow, and soon it would cut them off from the clearing!

There was no time to lose. Swiftly Kirstie ran to the edge of the pool. Obviously, the narrow channel between the rocks behind the waterfall had been blocked by driftwood and other debris, so the floodwater couldn't drain away into the stream that flowed across the clearing. Instead, it was rising rapidly over the ledge.

Telling Lucky to stay where he was, she waved both arms and yelled up at the figures on the cliff. 'Matt, Lisa; I'm going ahead into the clearing!'

Matt's reply was drowned by the sound of the waterfall. In any case, it made no difference. Nothing would stop her from checking on the black horse.

Kirstie stumbled and splashed through the pool, taking a short cut towards the vanishing ledge. Already soaked through, she hauled herself up and began to crawl behind the thundering fall. The water splashed white and foaming all around. Dark rock towered to one side; to the other was a wall of water.

She gasped and crawled on down the sloping

ledge. Water was tumbling on to her, bowing her under its force. She had to close her eyes, hold her breath, crawl on, until at last she reached the end of the ledge. Now she could squeeze into the narrow, water-filled gap between two rock-faces. She could fumble with her fingertips along the stone corridor, feeling the water hammering down on to her, resisting the rush of the stream as it tried to sweep her along.

But, before the end of the gulley, she found an obstacle blocking her way. It was as she thought; a heavy log had jammed across the gap, and a pile of stones and brushwood had collected against it. Water was building up behind the jam, which Kirstie would have to climb to get into the clearing. Steadying herself, feeling the current swirl around her legs and up to her waist, she dragged herself over the sodden barricade.

On the far side she eased herself down into the clearing. She pushed the wet hair from her face and took a deep breath. After the roar and crash of the waterfall came the peace and quiet, the green trees and grass, the black horse in the sunlight.

He stood by the stream as if waiting, his left leg

raised from the ground, head up, ears turned towards her.

So beautiful. Caught up in the spell of his powerful presence, Kirstie walked towards him. To her amazement and delight, the horse responded by stepping forwards; one, two, three paces. His injured left leg took his weight, his limp was much less than before. Kirstie smiled at the sight of the stallion's steady approach.

But only a few metres behind her, the flood-water was rising. She glanced back. The strong current pressed at the log jam, shifting stones, trickling through the gaps into the already swollen stream.

Then suddenly, as she was about to turn to the stallion and reassure him, the main log gave way. Kirstie heard the dam burst and the water rush through in a torrent. With a gasp she prepared to stand her ground.

The powerful wave roared at her and engulfed her, knocked her off her feet, swept her on. She went under, flung out her arms, tried to grab at something solid as the current twisted and turned her. She came up, dragged air into her lungs, sought to save herself.

The stallion was her only hope. He stood in the path of the surging stream. Water swirled around his legs, his chest. It swept Kirstie directly towards him. She closed her outstretched arms around his neck, felt him lose his footing and slide into the water with her.

Then he was floating. She was clinging to his neck, the horse's magnificent head was clear of the water and he was swimming through the flood, carrying her to safety.

10

The stallion's strength lifted Kirstie clear of danger. She clung to him, clutching at his mane until his feet found solid ground. The water tugged at her, testing her grasp, but she held fast, felt the horse stand firm, then managed to straddle his back as he stepped out of the raging flood.

When he reached dry land, she found herself slumped forward, her head against his wet black mane, her arms still circling his powerful neck.

Kirstie breathed out with a sob and a groan. In

the instant when the cold floodwater had closed over her head, she'd faced death. A moment's noisy confusion, then clarity and silence, before she'd put her arms around the horse and been saved.

'That was a pretty neat piece of luck,' a voice said.

She looked up and all around. The voice had belonged to a stranger, not to Matt or Lisa or Lennie Goodman. Bob Tyson then? She tried to match The Drifter's low, mean tones with the voice she'd just heard.

'You could say that horse just saved your life.'

A figure was walking towards her as she slid quietly from the stallion's back. She could see a man's legs as she crouched beside the horse; legs in jeans and cowboy boots.

'I guess that evens things up. You dig him out from under a heap of rocks. He saves you from drowning.' The voice was light, even amused. The booted feet came to a halt a few metres from them. 'Kinda neat, like I said.'

Kirstie stood up and stepped to one side of the stallion. She shivered and dripped as she came face to face with the one witness to the stallion's courage.

'Art Fischer.' The man held out a hand for her to shake. 'I would'a helped too, only I was too far off.'

She stared at the hand, then the checkered padded jacket. She looked up at a pair of brown eyes in a smiling face; smiling as if she hadn't nearly drowned back there.

'You saw me yesterday by Hummingbird Rock,' he reminded her. 'Horseshoe Creek, remember?'

The man with the fishing-rod! 'Yep.' She nodded hard, sensing the black horse turn away from her and towards the man. 'We thought you were Bob Tyson ... that is, Lisa ... she heard a noise ... were you watching us?'

It was the man's turn to nod. The smile seemed to stay on his face, around his eyes, even though it had faded from his lips. 'Tyson moved on,' he told Kirstie.

'When?' The news was slow to sink in through the questions flying round inside her head.

'Midday. He gave up on the grey mare he wanted once the Forest Guards got on his case. Didn't stop to say too many goodbyes before he packed up his trailer and left.' Art Fischer watched and waited for the horse to leave Kirstie's side. He studied the injured leg as he limped slowly towards him.

'You told Smiley Gilpin?' Kirstie frowned. Slowly she puzzled out what had happened.

Art gave another slight nod. Gently he greeted the stallion by rubbing his long nose with the back of his hand.

'He lets you get pretty friendly, doesn't he?' She noticed that the stallion had no fear around Art.

'I guess.'

'You wouldn't say he was a wild horse to look ... at ... him now ...' Kirstie slowed down and tailed off. The stallion nuzzled Art's hand, then pushed at his chest with his dark muzzle. 'How come?'

Letting her work out the answer for herself, Art scratched the stallion's forehead and ran an expert hand along the animal's neck and across his shoulder. Then he stooped to examine the injured knee.

Kirstie watched the man inspect the wound to check that the swelling was down and the horse was able to bend the joint. She saw him reach into his jacket pocket and take out a tub of white cream. He unscrewed the lid, dipped in his fingertips and gently began to smear ointment on to the jagged cut.

'Art is the mystery healer!' Kirstie told Lisa.

Together she and the quiet stranger had made their way along the ledge behind the waterfall into Dead Man's Canyon.

Lisa stared as if she was seeng a ghost. 'We never thought you'd make it out of there!'

'Well, I did, thanks to the stallion. And listen, Art's the one who led him into the clearing first of all; not Bob Tyson!' Kirstie was dripping wet and shaking all over. 'Art's been taking care of him ever since the landslide. Isn't that great?'

Matt stepped forward to sling his jacket around her shoulders. 'Save it for later,' he said quietly. He squeezed her gently and kept one arm around her while she went on regardless.

'Tyson wasn't the only one who knows all the old stuff about horses. Art here picked it up from his grandpa when he was a little kid. His folks had a ranch over by Aspen Falls before they built the Interstate highway there. Then they moved away to Colorado Springs, but Art didn't like the city. He lives in a trailer up at Eden Lake. That's where he first saw the wild horses . . .'

'Whoa!' Art Fischer stopped staring at his wet boots, looked up and spoke for the first time. 'I didn't reckon on you telling them my whole life story.'

'But it's brilliant! You taught yourself the medicine stuff by working alongside your grandpa. And you've remembered all of it!' Art had explained everything in answer to her breathless questions in the clearing. Then, once he was satisfied that the unexpected swim hadn't done the horse too much harm, they'd left him in peace and quickly come back to the canyon.

'I guess. But no way do I want folks knocking on my door pestering me with damn fool questions,' he protested. 'I got a quiet life up by the lake, and that's the way I like it.'

Kirstie bit her lip and blushed. 'You're not mad at me?' To her, Art was her new hero. He might not look or sound like one, with his faded clothes, his shy way of hanging his head and his quiet, funny voice, but what he'd done for the black stallion made him number one in her eyes.

He smiled now and shook his head.

But, as if in answer to Art's fears that his privacy was about to be invaded, the sound of Lennie Goodman's bulldozer rumbling up Meltwater Trail broke the silence of the mountain. And up on the ridge, a group of trail-riders appeared with Hadley at their head. The line strung out along the cliff edge, staring down at the small group standing in the canyon.

'Hey, Art!' Hadley stood up in his stirrups and hollered. 'How are y'all?'

'Hey!' Art answered. He turned his head away from the onlookers, ducked his head and shrugged.

Kirstie stared from one to the other; the old wrangler on the ridge riding Yukon, her new friend standing by her side. 'You know him?' Cupping her hands to her mouth, she yelled up at Hadley.

'Sure I know him. He's Fenney Fischer's boy from Aspen Falls.'

'How come you didn't tell us?' she cried.

And back came the slow, inevitable answer, as Hadley led the riders on along the ridge: 'How come you never asked?'

'I got a real nice site at Lone Elm,' Lennie told Art later that same evening. The bulldozer had shifted tons of rock and earth, and the entrance to Dead Man's Canyon was clear at last. 'It's got running water, I can connect you up to the electricity generator, no problem.'

Art listened and smiled.

Lisa's grandpa described the advantages of moving down from lonely Eden Lake to the comforts of an official trailer park. 'Hot showers, a grocery store right on site, folks to get along with on a long winter's night.'

Kirstie raised her eyebrows at Lisa, slipped an arm through hers and wandered away from the group. She was happy that the blocked entrance had been cleared, glad that Matt had contacted their mom on the radio and that Sandy and Hadley had made it to the canyon with a set of dry clothes for Kirstie and in time to see Lennie's giant machine complete the job.

Now it was evening. The sun was setting, shadows creeping down the silent mountain.

'What do you reckon? Will Art take Grandpa's vacant site?' Lisa asked as they strolled towards the waterfall.

'Nope.' Kirstie grinned. 'Folks can come knocking too easy with their damn fool questions in a trailer park.'

Lisa glanced back at Art, standing now a little way apart from Matt and Sandy Scott, her grandpa and Hadley. 'He's kinda shy.'

'Kinda.' She took a deep breath and gazed up at the sparkling, rushing water. Beyond the fall, beyond Miners' Ridge and way past Eagle's Peak in the far distance, the sun was disappearing from the sky. 'He says dawn tomorrow we can let the stallion go free,' she told Lisa softly. 'Do you want to be here?'

Tuesday sunrise. Before the guests at Half-Moon Ranch were stirring, while Matt and Sandy, Hadley and Charlie were bringing in the horses from the ramuda, brushing them down and saddling them up for the day's rides, Kirstie rode out with Lisa to Dead Man's Canyon.

Though the sun was just up and the air still sharp with an overnight frost, Art Fischer was there before them.

'Hey,' he said quietly.

'Hey, Art.' The girls dismounted and tied up Lucky and Cadillac.

Then they all three went along the ledge behind the fall to bring the black stallion out of the clearing.

He was grazing by the young aspen trees. When he saw them, he came quietly, curiously, taking his weight nicely on the left front leg, the limp almost gone. Kirstie and Lisa held their breaths, and as he came close, they gazed up into his deep brown eyes.

He scarcely noticed when Art quietly slipped a halter rope around his neck. It tightened. He pulled away once, then accepted it.

Art spoke gently to him, rubbing the back of his hand up and down his long face. 'Easy, boy. Time for you to leave this place.'

The horse heard and followed the man along the

bed of the stream, out of the clearing between the tall rocks of the dark gulley. Not even the narrow ledge behind the waterfall spooked him. He just went straight along it, right after Art Fischer.

Lisa and Kirstie watched with silent awe the trust between horse and man.

'It's magic!' Lisa breathed as they came out into the canyon and saw Art prepare to release the stallion.

He turned to Kirstie. 'Say goodbye?'

She nodded and went forward, feeling tears prick her eyelids. A happy-sad goodbye. A good goodbye to a horse whose life she'd helped to save – and who had helped to save hers too. She reached out with a trembling hand to stroke his lovely face.

The stallion bowed his head.

Then Art led him towards the cleared exit. He loosened the halter rope and slipped it off.

'Bye,' Lisa whispered.

Kirstie stood silent.

Then Art tapped the horse's shoulder with the flat of his hand. He clicked with his tongue.

The stallion stepped forward, hesitated, looked back at them.

From up above, high on Miners' Ridge, a horse whinnied. It was the grey mare, standing in the morning sun, her white mane bright. Behind her, in the shadows of the ponderosa pines, the wild herd waited.

The black horse looked up. He pawed the earth with one front hoof, stretched out his magnificent head and called back.

Then he reared and whirled. He was gone; out through the narrow gap cleared by the machine, up on to the trail that led to the ridge. He loped

with the wind in his black mane and tail, dark against the red rocks, the tall green trees; like a shadow, like a dream . . .

He was gone.